"I thought you were going to comfort me."

Taylor's words messed with Mac's head, tempting him. He knew if he so much as touched her, he'd never stop. He took a deep breath, needing to put some distance between them.

"You're going to be fine." It was himself he was worried about at the moment.

As he watched, she shrugged her robe off, leaving her shoulders bare, leaving her body bare except for that column of silk and the ribbon beneath her breasts. Crossing her arms, she ran her hands up and down her arms and shivered. "It cooled off tonight."

Had it? He was hot as hell, sweating just watching her.

When she shivered again, he sighed, recognizing the inevitable, and took a step toward her.

The top of her gown dipped low, exposing the soft curves of her breasts. The material clung to her, molding and outlining every part of her that he'd been dying to touch, taste since he'd first seen her.

"Warm me up," she whispered.

His hands slid to her hips before he could stop himself. "Taylor—"

"No, don't think. Just touch me."

Dear Reader,

I had so much fun writing my first Harlequin mini-series—SOUTH VILLAGE SINGLES. I have to confess a particular soft spot for this story. The hero, Mac, is a deliciously sexy, alpha guy with a heart of gold. And whether he likes it or not, he's met his match with Taylor—a tough, brave woman who, for all her outrageous wit, isn't so sharp when it comes to men. Oh, boy, the fun I had pitting these two against each other!

I hope you enjoy their fall into love. If you haven't already, be sure to read the other Harlequin Temptation SOUTH VILLAGE SINGLES stories— #910 *Roughing It With Ryan* and #914 *Tangling With Ty*. Also, look for *Men of Courage,* a May 2003 anthology where I team up with Lori Foster and Donna Kauffman. And keep an eye out for my first single title, *The Street Where She Lives,* coming out in October 2003, when we return to South Village.

Happy reading!

Jill Shalvis

P.S. I'd love to hear from you about this or any of my other books. You can reach me at P.O. Box 3945, Truckee, CA 96161, or check out my new Web site at www.jillshalvis.com.

Books by Jill Shalvis

HARLEQUIN TEMPTATION
845—AFTERSHOCK
861—A PRINCE OF A GUY
878—HER PERFECT STRANGER
885—FOR THE LOVE OF NICK
910—ROUGHING IT WITH RYAN*
914—TANGLING WITH TY*

*South Village Singles

HARLEQUIN DUETS
28—NEW AND...IMPROVED?
42—KISS ME, KATIE!
    HUG ME, HOLLY!
57—BLIND DATE DISASTERS
    EAT YOUR HEART OUT
85—A ROYAL MESS
    HER KNIGHT TO
    REMEMBER

HARLEQUIN BLAZE
63—NAUGHTY BUT NICE

Jill Shalvis
MESSING WITH MAC

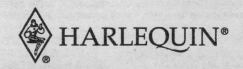

TORONTO • NEW YORK • LONDON
AMSTERDAM • PARIS • SYDNEY • HAMBURG
STOCKHOLM • ATHENS • TOKYO • MILAN • MADRID
PRAGUE • WARSAW • BUDAPEST • AUCKLAND

For Courtney,
for watching every Disney movie ever made ten times
during the writing of this book.

ISBN 0-373-69118-1

MESSING WITH MAC

Copyright © 2003 by Jill Shalvis.

All rights reserved. Except for use in any review, the reproduction or
utilization of this work in whole or in part in any form by any electronic,
mechanical or other means, now known or hereafter invented, including
xerography, photocopying and recording, or in any information storage
or retrieval system, is forbidden without the written permission of the
publisher, Harlequin Enterprises Limited, 225 Duncan Mill Road,
Don Mills, Ontario, Canada M3B 3K9.

All characters in this book have no existence outside the imagination of
the author and have no relation whatsoever to anyone bearing the same
name or names. They are not even distantly inspired by any individual
known or unknown to the author, and all incidents are pure invention.

This edition published by arrangement with Harlequin Books S.A.

® and TM are trademarks of the publisher. Trademarks indicated with
® are registered in the United States Patent and Trademark Office, the
Canadian Trade Marks Office and in other countries.

Visit us at www.eHarlequin.com

Printed in U.S.A.

1

ONE OF THESE DAYS, Taylor Wellington figured she'd be old, maybe even wrinkled, and then, finally then, her best friends would stop trying to convince her she needed love.

No one needed love.

Having been both with it and without it—mostly without it—she knew this for a cold, hard fact. Still, Taylor held the cell phone to her ear and let Nicole and Suzanne, via three-way conferencing, ramble on about how amazing the L-word was.

"You've got to try it." This from Nicole, who'd been swept off her feet a few months back by Ty Patrick O'Grady, Taylor's rebel Irish architect.

"It's even better than ice cream," Suzanne promised, and coming from Suzanne, this was quite the promise, but she'd recently fallen in love, too, and had even gone one step further and gotten married. "Come on, Taylor, give up on singlehood and try a man on for size. It'll change your life."

Taylor wasn't buying it. Not one little bit. In her opinion—and she had very strong opinions, thank you very much—love sucked. Always had, always would.

She was speaking from firsthand experience and hard-earned knowledge, not that her friends would understand. They wouldn't because she hadn't explained, she hadn't known how to in the short time they'd been together, which had begun when, in order to keep up with life's little luxuries like eating, Taylor had rented out two apartments in the building she'd just inherited. Suzanne had come first, then later Nicole, and both had happily joined her in a solemn vow of singlehood.

Only they'd each caved like cheap suitcases in the face of true love, and had both recently moved out again, having found their soul mates.

"Just because you two willingly gave up your freedom doesn't mean I have to—" Taylor stopped at an odd noise and cocked an ear. "Hang on a sec."

The building, *her* building, shuddered. Not surprising really, as she considered it an amazing feat the entire thing hadn't fallen down long ago, but in Taylor's world, things didn't happen off schedule. Her building crashing to the ground definitely wasn't on her schedule for today.

And yet there it went again. Another shudder. And then again. Something was systematically banging, in tune with her growing headache. "Guys, much as I'd love to listen to you tell me what's wrong with my life in singular excruciating detail, I have to run."

"Hold up. Is that more construction I hear?" Suzanne asked casually. *Too* casually.

The question didn't fool Taylor. Both Suzanne and Nicole had found their happiness due to construction. *Her* construction.

Now they had equally high hopes for her.

They were going to be disappointed, as Taylor didn't intend to fall for anyone. Feeling like a heel, she pulled the cell phone away from her ear and simulated a static sound with her mouth. It wasn't a kind thing to do to the only two people in the world who truly cared about her, but all this talk of love, no matter how well-meaning, was making her perspire.

And a Wellington never perspired, especially in silk. That was one thing she'd learned from her mother. "Gotta go, bad connection!" she yelled into the phone and disconnected.

Damn it. She loved Suzanne and Nicole, loved them like the sisters she'd always wished for instead of the two she had, but any more talk of love as it pertained to her and she risked losing her wits, something she couldn't afford at the moment, as she needed each and every available wit to keep her sane.

Oh, and in the black. Her every thought these days seemed to focus on finding enough money to pay for the work that needed to be done. That alone was enough to give her insomnia. This was a real kicker of an inheritance from her grandfather—this falling-off-its-foundation building she stood in, and not a single penny to go with it. No trust fund, no cushy little savings account, nothing.

After a lifetime of paying for all her fancy education and everything else, the distant, cruel bastard had cut her off cold turkey, giving all of his substantial wealth to her mother, who hadn't seen fit to share.

The woman wouldn't, not when all her life she'd been so cheap, so tight with money, she squeaked when she walked.

Well, tough. Taylor wouldn't wallow over that, or the fact that her family—called such only because they shared the same bloodlines—probably wouldn't notice if she succeeded, but would most definitely notice if she failed. And she wouldn't think about the fact that she only had to sell this place and walk away if she chose, because sheer stubborn pride refused to allow her to walk away from the first real challenge in her life.

She would do this. She would take this place and make something of it. And of herself. She'd started months ago, one room at a time, but had decided to sell several of her precious antiques—which had been worth more than she'd imagined—using the opportunity to renovate all of it in one fell swoop.

Starting tomorrow.

Hard as it would be to maintain her notorious cool, maintain it she would. With a nod of determination, she slipped the phone into her pocket and narrowed her eyes at the walls, which were still quivering from the rhythmic blows.

Oh, yes, she was quite certain she'd agreed with her new contractor that he could start tomorrow.

Not today.

And if there was one thing Taylor didn't appreciate, it was someone messing with her carefully laid plans. She needed today, her last day alone, her last day to buck up, thrust out her chin, and get ready to show the world what she was made of.

Her building had been built circa 1902, and looked liked it. The Victorian style had nooks and crannies everywhere, windows galore and all the old charm and personality from the turn of the previous century, but with a hundred years of neglect added in. To say it was falling apart was the understatement of the new millennium. Bad trim, bad siding, bad paint, bad electrical and never mind the termites and last year's flood damage from a busted pipe.

The bottom floor had two store-front units. The top floor had one loft apartment and an attic compartment. The middle floor had two apartments, one of which she'd claimed. Shutting the door of her apartment now, she headed downstairs, toward the hideous banging.

Outside, the streets of South Village were gearing up for what promised to be another profitable day. Los Angeles, only five miles away, had been kind enough to share its smog and muggy heat, but Taylor didn't mind the summer months like so many others did. She loved it here, felt perfectly at home among the young, hip, urban crowd which was drawn to Southern California's premier pedestrian neighborhood. And why not, when any day of the week one could walk to a theater, an outdoor café run by someone famous or simply stroll through a mecca of interesting galleries or shops.

Taylor was counting on that crowd, as someday soon her two storefronts would be ready for lease. Suzanne was taking one of them for her catering business, she'd already committed to that. A relief. But there was still the other one. Leasing it out would keep her bank account happier than it was at the moment. But the truth was, she'd held out a little tiny seed of hope that someday she could use it for herself, opening her own shop. That is, if she had any antiques left after using them to finance the renovation.

A definite pipe dream at the moment.

The banging sounded louder now, and was definitely coming from one of the dusty, dirty storefront units. Outside, from beyond the front gate, she could hear people walking by, talking, laughing. Shopping. Once upon a time, that had been her favorite pastime, shopping, and a silly part of her suddenly yearned to be out there.

But that, too, was for another day.

As she reached the left unit, the banging increased in intensity. Opening the hallway door, which led into the back, she was greeted with a thick cloud of dust. The banging was so loud now she could hardly hear herself think, but as she stepped inside, the noise abruptly stopped.

Stunned by the silence, Taylor inhaled dirt in the already hot, muggy, spring California morning, and wondered how long before her carefully curled hair, flowing in a purposely artful and loose manner beneath her straw hat, sagged into her face.

"You're in my way," said a low, gruff voice from behind her.

Whirling, Taylor blinked into the cloud of dust as it slowly settled. Standing there among the dirt and grime was a man. He had one long arm propped on his hip, the other holding a huge sledgehammer, which rested against his shoulder.

Paul Bunyan, came the inane thought, if one substituted the sledgehammer for an ax. But why was Paul Bunyan standing in her building? Confused, a rare occurrence for Taylor, she found herself momentarily speechless.

Another rare occurrence.

The dust started to settle, and Paul materialized into her contractor Thomas Mackenzie, and though most of their contact had been handled by e-mail and telephone, she *had* seen him before. Clean and dressed up, that is. He wasn't clean or dressed up now.

At least four inches taller than her own willowy five-foot-ten frame, she found it a bit of a surprise to have to tip her head back to see his face. The last time she'd seen him, they'd sat at her table, and for the life of her, she didn't remember him being so...tall, so built, so imposing.

His mouth was scowling. His eyes were the color of expensive whiskey, two liquid, shining pools of heat and annoyance, and his hair, an exact match to his eyes, fell over a blue bandanna which had been tied around his forehead. Combined with his unsmiling, and rough and tumble expression, he looked more than just a little dangerous.

At the thought, a completely inappropriate shiver of thrill raced down her spine. Now was not the greatest time to remember that while she'd vowed to remain single for the rest of her life, she'd never vowed to remain celibate. She had a great appreciation for all things beautiful and finely made. And this man—tall and edgy and frowning as he was— was beautifully and firmly made, a magnificent male specimen, one who seemed to awaken every hormone and nerve ending in her entire body.

But she most definitely did not have a thing for a rebel-at-heart, and it didn't escape her that this man was one-hundred-percent pure attitude.

In light of that, she repeated the same thing she told herself at estate sales, when she saw some spectacular piece of furniture she quivered to own but couldn't afford... Walk away. Just walk away. Repeating that mantra, she took a careful step backward, taking one last glimpse to tide her over.

Hard, powerful looking legs were encased in soft, faded denim. His work boots were well worn, with a sole made for the long haul. She'd already noticed his very capable arms and his chest, which was wide, hard and covered in a T-shirt that clung like a second skin to his damp body. He was long and lean, rugged and virile, the way she preferred a man, when she chose to be with one.

But she wasn't choosing now.

"You're still in my way," he said.

"Good morning to you, too, Mr. Mackenzie."

He blew out a breath. "Mac."

"What?"

"You can call me Mac. That's my name."

"Really? It's not Mr. Attitude?"

His lips twitched. "I respond better to Mac."

"Okay, then. Mac."

He stood there politely enough, and...waited for something. At his raised brow, she realized he was waiting for her to leave.

Too bad he didn't know her better, or he'd already know she did only as she pleased, not as expected. "I didn't approve for the demo to begin today," she said.

"You signed the contract."

Yes, she had. She'd sold her beloved Queen Anne headboard to give him the first payment of many, but she'd agreed upon tomorrow. Damn it, she needed today.

Apparently deciding they were done, Mac turned and walked away, moving with the easy, loose-limbed stride of a man who knew the value of patience. With that patience, he hoisted up the sledgehammer and brought it down on the south wall. And then again. His arms strained and stretched, his muscles working in perfect synch, taut and sleek with sweat as he completely ignored her while simultaneously stripping down the wall to the framing.

Unable to help herself, she stared, utterly fascinated by the unrestrained violence of what he was doing. By the hone of that well-built machine that was his body. "Um...excuse me?"

The sledgehammer continued to rise and fall with amazing regularity. What kind of strength did that entail, she wondered, watching with utter fascination as Mac's muscles flexed and flowed. Another shiver wracked her frame, and it had nothing to do with a chill. The room was hot. He was hot...and so, suddenly, was she.

Definitely, it had been too long since she'd had any sort of physical release besides her handy, dandy, trusty vibrator. "Mac?"

He never even looked at her, which was a bit disconcerting. Taylor had matured at an early age, her long, gangly body turning into a man's wet dream. In all the years since, she'd never failed to turn a head.

And yet she was being completely ignored now. Vexing. So was the cell phone ringing in her pocket. Pulling it out, she put it to one ear, finger in the other to hear over Mac, and yelled, "*Hello?*"

"I have bad news," said Mrs. Cabot, the owner of a very upscale antique shop in town.

"Bad news?"

Sledgehammer raised, Mac turned.

Their gazes locked.

It was like a chemical reaction. Unintended. Unavoidable. He had the most amazing eyes, and for the first time in her life, Taylor lost her place in a conversation. Chewing her lower lip, she wracked her brain for working brain cells, but her pulse tripled when Mac's gaze dropped from hers, and locked on the movement of her mouth.

This wasn't happening. He wasn't attracted to her. She wasn't attracted to him. That would be bad, very bad, but while she'd promised herself to never again engage her heart after the devastating loss she'd once suffered, she was no monk.

But even so, sex had become a very fond, distant memory.

She licked her lips, a nervous habit. Again, her contractor's gaze flickered downward, becoming hot, focused and filled with frank sexual curiosity.

Oh boy. With sheer will power, she concentrated on her phone conversation. "What's the bad news?"

Mac set the sledgehammer on the floor. In deference to her call? No, that would mean he had a considerate streak.

He was probably just done.

"I'm sorry," Mrs. Cabot said. "But you lost your bid on that nineteenth-century chandelier."

Instantly forgetting about Mac, she gripped the phone. "What do you mean? Who else bid on the chandelier?"

"You were outbid by..." Papers rustled. "Isabel W. Craftsman."

Taylor might have guessed. There was only one person in town who would have coveted that piece as much as she had, and that was her own mother.

It only had been Taylor's greatest heart's desire to own it, but hey, she figured her mother knew that, too. Her mother was highly educated, incredibly brilliant and had eyes in the back of her head. Bottom line, she knew everything, she always had.

Well, except how to be a mother. Shocking how she'd screwed that up, but maybe Taylor was partly to blame. She'd always resented her mother's vicious drive, sharp ambition and ability to multitask everything in her world except when it came to her own daughters.

When Taylor had graduated from college and had moved out of the house, she'd decided to be the grown-up and let it all go. She'd told her mother so, saying she'd forgiven her for all the missed events, the forgotten birthdays, the lack of any physical attention whatsoever. She didn't know what she expected, but it hadn't been to be cut off by her mother's cell phone. Her mother had held up a hand to Taylor, answered the call, dealt with some business problem, then absently kissed the air somewhere near Taylor's cheek and walked away.

Having completely forgotten they were in the middle of an important conversation.

After standing there in seething resentment, Taylor had shrugged and moved on. She'd had to. Not every mother was cut out to be a warm, fuzzy type, and she needed to get over it.

Then a few years ago Isabel had done the unthinkable, she'd gotten married again, and had dropped everything for one equally ambitious, equally cold-blooded Dr. Edward Craftsman, brain surgeon. Taylor had gone to the wedding, and if she hadn't seen it with her own eyes, she would never have believed it.

Her mother lived for this man, gushing all over him. Constantly. Kissing, hugging, leaning, more kissing.

It burned just thinking about it. So did her mother buying this chandelier from beneath her. "Thank you," Taylor said into the phone. And as if it were no skin off her nose, she dropped the phone back into her pocket. Damn it. Damn it, damn it, *damn it*. She'd wanted that chandelier with a ridiculous passion.

Served her right, wanting something so badly. Hadn't she learned that nothing, nothing at all, was worth the heartache?

She had other things to worry about. Like she had a building in disrepair, and a man was reminding her of things far better forgotten.

Mac had tossed the sledgehammer aside, but he hadn't been idle. There was now a shovel in his hand and he was loading debris into a wheelbarrow with the same narrow-minded intensity he'd swung his sledgehammer.

Eyes narrowed, she set her hands on her hips and tapped her foot. "We never solved the problem of why you're here a day early."

He kept loading until the wheelbarrow was full to bursting. Slowly he straightened, then eyed her with that light brown gaze, completely inscrutable now, without a trace of that intense sexual speculation.

Had she only imagined it?

"I didn't think twenty-four hours would make any difference to you," he said. Tossing the shovel aside, he grasped the handles of the wheelbarrow and lifted. Muscles strained. Tendons corded.

Taylor tore her gaze away. "I needed this last day before the hell of the next three months of construction and renovation. You've ruined it."

He swiped a forearm across his forehead, looking

tired, sweaty and temperamental. "I think that phone call ruined it."

Deep within her, a pesky lone hormone quivered. "I'd really like you to go and come back tomorrow."

That got his attention. "You're kidding, right?"

"No."

"You need to be alone bad enough to disrupt the start of your own renovation?"

"I do, yes."

"Fine." Dropping the wheelbarrow, he propped his hands on his hips. "Have your way, Princess. Tomorrow it is, but don't even think about pulling this again. I'm not going to postpone this job further, no matter what kind of day you're having."

Princess? Had he just called her *Princess*? She'd show him princess! Reaching up, she yanked off her wide-brimmed hat, which once upon a time had cost her—make that her grandfather—a bundle. She'd die before explaining that her fair skin required she protect it from the harsh summer sun, especially since he seemed like a man to mock such a weakness. "Tomorrow will be just fine," she said through her teeth, hat in her fist.

Mac stretched his shoulders, which put a strain on his T-shirt, not that she was noticing, and rubbed his eyes. "Good. I'm outta here. But since I am, and since steam is still coming out your ears, why don't you do both of us a favor." Retrieving the sledgehammer, he held it out. "Start pounding walls. Consider it anger management."

She stared down at the tool, having never in her life so much as lifted a screwdriver. She might have blamed her uptight, pretentious family for that, though she'd been on her own for awhile now, and could have made the effort to learn such things.

Should have, because it would feel good to swing the thing with authority and knowledge, surprising that smirk off his face.

He wriggled the sledgehammer enticingly.

Odd how a little part of her tingled to touch it, hoist it over her head and let loose. Barbaric, yes, and suddenly very appealing.

"You know you want to," Mac said in a low, husky dare. "Touch it."

She cocked a brow and looked at him from beneath lowered lashes. "So...are they all the same size?"

His eyes sparked, heated and flamed.

And one question was answered...she had most definitely *not* imagined that intense sexual speculation.

"I thought size didn't matter to a woman."

She lifted a shoulder. "That's just the story some

woman started in order to appease her poor husband who didn't have...the right equipment."

"Hmm." He lifted the sledgehammer again, his
eyes amused now. "The right equipment, huh?"

"That's right."

He looked at the sledgehammer with a new light,
then back into her eyes. "Seeing as I have the right
equipment, are you going to go for it?"

Oh yeah, she was. For the sledgehammer, anyway.

What could it hurt? She had aggression coming
out her ears; for her grandfather, who was probably
sitting on a cloud laughing down at her right this
very minute, for her mother, who would rather do
anything than be a mother, for her dwindling bank
account, for the chandelier she'd lost out on...for being alone in all this.

For just about every damn thing in her entire life,
she needed that sledgehammer.

Mac held it out.

Her fingers itched.

His eyes sizzled with the dare, and a potent, heady
male heat.

"Fine." She set her hat back on her head, snatched
the tool from him, then swore in a very unladylike
way as the thing jerked both her arms down with its
weight, slamming the heavy sledgehammer to the
floor.

Mac tsked. "Sorry, I thought you were stronger
than that."

2

TAYLOR'S ACCUSING EYES speared Mac, and he had to bite back his grin as he lifted an innocent shoulder.

She let out a rude sound, and with determination and aggression blaring out her eyes, she hoisted the sledgehammer up...and nearly fell to her very finely dressed ass. Stumbling back a step, she spread her legs out a little for balance, then sent him a triumphant smile.

It stopped his heart.

Funny, that, since he'd have sworn the organ in question had dried up from abuse and misuse.

Taylor turned her back on him and with all her might, swung the sledgehammer into the wall. When drywall fell and dust rose, she let out a cocky laugh, whirling back to make sure he was looking.

Oh, he was looking. He'd been looking since she'd first sauntered into the room, just as he had a feeling men always looked at Taylor Wellington.

He'd bet his last dollar that she knew it as well. She was a pricey number, all fancy labels and perfect grooming. Stunning, too, with her blond hair, see-through green eyes and a body meant to bring a grown man right to his knees. She had long, willowy curves, outlined in mouthwatering detail beneath the silky sundress that made his hands itch to mess her up. It was crazy, but he had the most inane urge to toss off her hat, sink his fingers into her hair and shake a little, to eat off her carefully applied lipstick that smelled like peaches and cream, to run his hands over that cobalt silk and see if she looked as good undone as she looked done.

But he recognized a spoiled socialite when he saw one. Oh yeah, he did. He'd been there, bought the T-shirt, and because of it, he wasn't tempted.

Well, maybe a little tempted, but he wasn't an idiot. She was upset because of some silly little bid she'd lost for a damn light fixture, when Mac had his entire future riding on a bid as well. A bid with South Village's town council to get in on the area's renovation and preservation acts. South Village wasn't some prefab pedestrian neighborhood like Universal's City Walk, but a genuine historical district in the middle of extensive restoration. He had bid on several of the upcoming jobs that would hopefully set up his business and reputation. Now *that* was something to get a little excited over, and he was trying not to think about how badly he wanted to be awarded those bids.

Taylor lifted the sledgehammer again, and with all her might, gave it everything she had. Not a strand of hair fell out of place beneath her hat, and nary a wrinkle appeared on those fine clothes. More interesting, he sensed she wasn't just humoring him here, but was genuinely striving to work off steam. Her mouth was grim, her eyes quite focused on the task, as if she was imagining someone's face right where the sledgehammer fell.

It shocked him, the barely restrained violence pouring out of her, but what really shocked him was how arousing it was to watch her go at it. With every swing, her perfect, palm-sized breasts jiggled, her hips wriggled, her ass shimmied and shook.

And damn, but he couldn't tear his eyes away. "Remind me to never piss you off," he said, and she let out a rough sound of agreement as she swung again.

She was going to get blisters if she kept it up, which she appeared to intend to do. He hadn't expected her to be able to lift the sledgehammer, much less swing it. "Uh...Princess? Don't you think that's probably enough?"

Ignoring him, she swung again, but it took a huge effort.

Figuring she had to be nearing exhaustion, he shifted closer, thinking he should grab the sledgehammer before she hurt herself. That's all he needed, was to maim the boss before she paid him.

Blocking him with an elbow, she growled, "Back off."

Torn between annoyance and amusement, he did. "Okay, maybe I was wrong, maybe anger management classes would have been more effective for you."

"No." Heave. Smash. Heave. Smash. "You were right, this is good. And..." Heave. Smash. "Cheap, too."

She paused, gasping for breath.

"You could always just ask Daddy for more money," he suggested.

She went utterly still. Then carefully and purposely set down the sledgehammer before turning to him, eyes suddenly cold as ice. "You know, I think I'm finished after all. Thank you," she added politely, and then cool as he pleased, walked past him and quietly shut the door behind her.

Shaking his head, he let out a low whistle. Classy down to the last millimeter, when what she'd obviously wanted was to tear into his hide. Still in that state of amused annoyance, he let himself out of the unit as well, figuring he'd give in on this, her need to have the rest of the day to herself.

Only because it suited him.

Mac got into his truck and drove east. He didn't live in the high-class, high-rent district of South Village. Nor with the middle class in their gated condo developments and upscale houses that all mirrored each other. He didn't live with the wannabes on the outskirts either.

He lived exactly where he wanted to, and damn expectations. He lived in the area known as The Tracks, which before the Town Council and Historical Society had gotten a hold of it meant that he lived on the *wrong* side of the tracks.

He appreciated the irony of it.

In ten minutes he was walking into his own little house, *little* being the key word here. The first thing he did was toss his mail—unread—on the table, where it knocked over the existing pile of unpaid bills.

Didn't matter. No matter how big that stack got, he was still free. Free of his family's obligations, well-meaning but smothering nonetheless. Free of his ex-wife—whom he had to thank for all those unpaid bills.

He'd refused to let her live off his very generous family and their money, refused to make her the socialite she wanted to be. As a result, she'd taken everything he owned and then some before purposely and completely destroying him in the only way she could.

By aborting his child.

But he wasn't going there, not tonight. He stripped, hunted up a pair of beat-up old shorts and headed back out for his own anger management class.

A long, punishing run.

AT THE CRACK OF DAWN the next morning, Mac drove back to Taylor's building. He had a soft spot for this hour, before the sun had fully risen on the horizon, as no one had yet screwed up his day.

Today he'd have a crew working on the demolition, tearing out drywall down to the wood studs, then stripping old electrical and plumbing lines. Yesterday had been just for him, a way to burn off some accumulated steam. And he'd had plenty of it. There'd been that call from his mother, who in spite of her own life and full-time, very demanding job, was warm and loving and more than a little certain he was wasting away without her home cooking, and when was he going to come home for a Sunday meal?

Then had come the call from his old captain, wanting him back on the police force, which he'd left at the same time as his divorce four years ago. Much as

Mac had loved being a cop, he loved rebuilding and renovating more, and always had. He'd been building things, working with his hands, ever since he could remember, and his love of doing so hadn't changed.

But his purpose had. Life was too damn short, as he'd learned the hard way, and he intended to spend the rest of it doing what he loved. And what he loved was taking old, decrepit, run-down historical buildings and restoring them to their former glory. He'd been doing just that since getting off the force and had never looked back. He'd started out working for a friend of the family, learning the trade. For two years now, he'd been on his own doing mostly single rooms within existing buildings until this last year when he'd taken on whole buildings for the first time.

He'd found his calling. Taylor was his biggest client to date, his biggest job and his stepping stone to the next level.

He hoped. Thanks to Ariel, who'd dragged him through the coals financially, morally and every other way possible, he couldn't afford to renovate his own place, not yet. Fine. He'd do it for someone else and work his way up. He had no problem with that.

And with that single-mindedness, he parked right

in front of Taylor's building—a miracle given the deplorable parking in South Village—and fervently hoped she'd made herself scarce. He had a crew to think about, and he wanted their minds on work, not on a beautiful woman, no matter how good she'd looked swinging a sledgehammer in all her finery.

His crew was waiting for him, just standing on the front steps, which made no sense. They knew better than to stand around wasting time.

But they weren't just standing, they were smiling and nodding like little puppets to...surprise, surprise...Taylor.

"It came from Russia," she was saying, holding up some sort of vase as he strode up the walk, annoyance already starting to simmer.

Taylor stroked perfectly manicured fingers over the smooth, porcelain surface of the vase as she talked, caressing the thing like she would a lover, and Mac's blood began to beat thick, and not with just annoyance now. An ache, purely sexual, began to spread through his belly.

Which proved it, he was insane.

"It's worth a small fortune," Taylor said, seeming lost in the delicate etching on the vase, sighing over the beauty of it as she touched.

The sound of her soft sigh didn't help Mac's inner ache, and he spent a moment brooding over the fact he hadn't been with a woman in a good long while. He hadn't wanted to, not since Ariel and her cruel betrayal.

But not having a sexual urge wasn't the same as ignoring one. He looked at the vase in Taylor's hands and concentrated on her words.

Worth a fortune, she'd said.

Enough to cover the wasted labor for however long she stood there occupying his men's every thought?

But what did she care how much money he lost in wages unearned? Mac wasn't exactly sure what had happened yesterday, why she'd momentarily drawn him, given who and what she was—that being a woman too close to Ariel's type to make him comfortable. But whatever it was, whatever little spark or electrical current of attraction he'd felt in spite of himself, he wouldn't feel again.

She wore a pair of pale blue capris with a matching short, little cropped jacket, looking like she should be getting ready to walk down the runway instead of standing on the step of her ugly building. Her hair was pulled back in a careful twist and she wore more of that peach lip-gloss from yesterday.

She was a long, cool drink of water, and even knowing it, even having prepared himself to see her again, he was suddenly dying of thirst, and couldn't seem to tear his eyes off her.

When she saw him, she stopped talking, rubbing her lips together in a little gesture that signified either nerves or arousal. Either way, awareness shot straight to his groin.

So much for ignoring her. "Why are you here?" he asked.

She lifted a brow, assuring him and everyone around that she considered him a Neanderthal for asking such a question. And okay, yes, maybe his tone had been a bit brusque. After all, she did own the place. But there was some inexplicable...*thing* going on between the two of them, some amazing thing that reminded him of...a shark bite. Painful, and probably lethal.

But they'd signed a contact, he and she. Every possible little detail had been decided on, down to the last shade of paint on the walls. Her presence here wasn't required, and in fact, he knew the ratio of work done today would be directly related to how far away she was.

The further the better. "You agreed to move out for the duration of the restoration," he reminded her.

"I agreed to make sure there were no tenants during the duration. Suzanne and Nicole are gone."

"But you're not."

"I'm not a tenant."

Shaking his head, he took the last step that put him on even ground with her. Mostly he towered over everyone around him, and knowing it, he usually made a conscious effort not to use his size as an intimidation. But right now he wasn't thinking intimidation so much as self-preservation. He wanted this job. He needed this job. It was the first thing he'd cared about in far too long. And in a way he was just beginning to understand, he needed to lose himself in the pure joy of the work itself, something he couldn't do with her parading around all damn day. "You can't mean to be here while we work."

She lifted that chin, eyes flashing. "I'll do as I please."

Damn. She did, she meant to be here while they worked. Because she didn't trust him, or because she wanted to drive him crazy every step of the way? "Why?"

"I won't be in your way," she said in lieu of a real answer.

In his experience, clients couldn't help but be in the way, always wanting to change the logical order of things, waiting until paint was on the walls or tile on the floor before deciding the color was off, or the brand not quite right. And he had the Town Council and historical society to impress on this one. "Look, Princess—"

"My name," she said, still smiling that cool smile as she carefully shifted the vase from one hand to the other in a way that suggested she was considering smashing it over his head, "is not 'Princess.'"

He pinched the bridge of his nose. "I'm not trying to be a hard-ass here, it's just that we'd all be better off if you'd just let us do our jobs."

"You *are* a hard-ass, it's one of the reasons I hired you," she said, surprising him. "And I think you could try trusting me a little. I'm not going to bog you down."

Mac didn't do trust, and even if he did, he'd be crazy to give in to a woman quite used to crooking her little finger and having the entire male population fall over its own feet to please her.

"I'm not," she repeated, a little softer now, watching him with those clear, clear eyes that weren't going to give an inch.

He ran his hands over his face, put them on his hips and stared at her, but she was still just waiting with what he figured was the patience of a cobra. "Okay, whatever."

She was wise enough to keep her smile to herself but he saw the triumph in her eyes, the eyes that only yesterday had turned him on.

Still turned him on.

"You'll finish the demo downstairs this week?" she asked.

"And upstairs."

"Oh." Now something else flickered in her gaze. "Is it really necessary to push your men like that?"

"Like...what?"

"Well, I would think demolishing just the downstairs would be enough for the next week. In any case, it's going to be awfully hot."

"We're doing both up and down this week," he said firmly.

"Hmm."

The sound that escaped her throat suggested he was not only a hard-ass but a brutal boss to his crew. "Demolition is back-breaking, hot, filthy work," he explained, trying not to resent having to do so.

"I realize that."

"Then you also realize we're far better off digging in and getting it over with quick as possible."

"Okay...well, maybe you guys can start and complete the entire renovation *downstairs* before moving to the next floor."

"No. Not cost-effective."

"Hmm," she said again doubtfully, and he narrowed his eyes. Why didn't she want them upstairs this week? He would have pushed for answers but each of his crew's heads were whipping back and forth between the two of them as if they were watching a tennis match.

He was not going to make a scene. The woman wanted to breathe down his neck all day long? Fine. Today was going to be particularly brutal. By the end of it, her hair would be in her face, her creamy skin smeared with dirt and no way was that million dollar linen going to make it through unscathed.

She'd be, at the very least, hot, sweaty and rumpled, and he could only hope he would get that insane urge to see it right out of his system.

"Let's move it," he said to his crew, and they scattered.

3

FOR SEVERAL DAYS, Taylor kept close tabs on the demolition, from a safe distance of course. She wasn't stupid enough to rile the beast any further, though she had to admit, she had been able to rile him with little to no effort so far.

She supposed that meant he felt the same irritating physical attraction she did. And it *was* purely physical. A man as alpha as Mac was only good for the physical. There was nothing sensitive, tender or gentle about a man like that, nothing.

He wasn't someone to fool around with. He'd swallow her whole and spit her right back out, and in her world, *she* was the one who did the spitting, thank you very much.

What she needed, if she needed at all, was a far more beta man to have fun with, to walk all over, if that's what she was looking for.

And maybe she would. Later. Right now she had bigger problems, such as figuring out how to keep her contractor from learning she wasn't just going to be casually around, she was still living here.

Not because she didn't trust him, as he figured, but because she didn't have the money to move out and get another place. Every cent she had was sunk into this building and the renovations. Until she could get more tenants—something else she was dependent on her contractor for—she was pretty much stuck.

Suzanne and Nicole had each offered her a place to stay. But Nicole lived in Ty's house now, and Suzanne with Ryan. Both were deliciously, deliriously drunk on true love. She knew the feeling, oh yes, she knew, but she couldn't watch it or witness it too closely. She just couldn't.

She figured she'd just stay here, quietly, out of the way.

Undetected.

But that would be tricky, because now she knew the truth, that very little, and quite possibly nothing, got past one Thomas Mackenzie.

"You want to move, Princess, or you'll feel the effects of this dust in two seconds flat."

Having come out of nowhere, the tall, moody, opinionated man in question stood at the bottom of the stairs, looking up at her. She leaned against the railing on the second-floor landing just outside her apartment, the one he didn't realize she still slept in.

He wore a hard hat, protective goggles and a face

mask, which he'd shoved off his mouth, and was now hanging around his neck. He also wore a fine layer of dust that clung to his damp body. So did his dark T-shirt, which she was quite certain shouldn't make her pulse quicken. He seemed so huge, so powerful and virile standing there with his sledge-hammer in hand as he stared up at her from those whiskey eyes. And ridiculous as it was, she quivered like a mare in heat. It was shockingly, amazingly juvenile, and if she'd known how it was going to be, she'd have found another man for the job.

No, scratch that, difficult as he was, she wouldn't want to work with anyone else. He was abrupt, insensitive and far too hardheaded, but he was a damn good contractor and he was honest to a fault.

Honest or otherwise, he slowly climbed the stairs, holding her gaze in his, until he stood right before her, all but surrounding her with his size and strength in what she considered was a deliberate attempt to establish his dominance.

Well, she was dominant, too, and she lifted her chin and stared him down.

"You're not moving out of the dust," he said.

She wouldn't back up, not even one little step, though he was close enough now that she could feel the heat of his body, could see the look in his light brown eyes, and it was a very confident, cocksure look.

Even her heartbeat responded to his nearness, quickening, causing a glowing, growing heat within her body. Combined with the almost frantic awareness humming through her every nerve ending, she felt like a bomb waiting to go off.

No. She couldn't be attracted to him, he wasn't what she wanted in a man. He wasn't quiet, easygoing. He wasn't laid-back. And he certainly wouldn't let her walk all over him.

Damn, but it had been a long time since a man had gotten to her like this, really gotten to her. And to be fair, Jeff Hathaway had been more boy than man.

They'd met in second grade. Jeff had slugged Tony Villa for calling her a Jolly Green Giant when she'd worn a green dress and green tights with matching green patent leather shoes, and even back then Taylor's heart had sighed.

In sixth grade Jeff held her hand at lunch break, not caring who saw, and her heart had sighed again and again.

By high school, they'd been soul mates. She'd known he was the one, no matter that he came from what her mother had called an undesirable family. Jeff *was* her family.

They'd wanted to get married right out of high

school but she hadn't turned eighteen and her mother wouldn't give her permission. So they plotted away the summer, talking about college, where they'd room together, and then sneak off to Vegas when she turned eighteen in October.

By that time, Jeff had been her best friend, her lover, her future husband and her entire life.

And on the last day of September, he'd been killed in a car accident.

Those days immediately following, and even several years after, didn't bear thinking about. But always having been strong of heart, Taylor did eventually heal. She even moved on, and dated a little in her early twenties, when fast, fun and reckless were infinitely preferable to deep and emotional.

Even now at twenty-seven, she felt perfectly normal, but a part of her was missing. The best part. Jeff.

God, she'd loved him. Oh, she could still function, could even care about a man. She could laugh and learn and do all the things she'd done before.

But one thing had irrevocably changed. Now when she let a man in, it was simply to soothe a need, whether it be wanting to be held against his hard body, or merely needing a sexual release that didn't come from something battery operated.

Nothing more, nothing less, as even now, nearly

ten years later, she couldn't imagine going through that soul-destroying love ever again.

"Princess?"

How could she have forgotten the very unforgettable man looking at her? The one man since Jeff she'd actually found herself yearning for.

There. The admission was out in the open, not that she was going to do anything about it. He was not, repeat *not*, her type. "I'm not allergic to a bit of dust."

"You haven't been breathing it in. Continue to stand there while we demo the hallway and your lungs will be burning within half an hour. Not to mention the pounding sinus headache that accompanies it."

Was that concern? If so, it didn't bear thinking about, as it might soften her toward him. And given her body's response to his without letting her brain get into the mix, that would be just plain stupid. And dangerous.

"Thanks for the concern," she said sweetly, and turned away. She entered her apartment, stripped now of all furnishings and personal belongings except for the bedroom. Everything had been taken to her storage unit, where she also kept her precious antiques.

But here, in her private sanctuary, her bedroom,

she still had her huge four-poster bed and the luxurious beddings left over from the good old days before the end of her bottomless—and now nearly extinct—bank account.

She wasn't upset she had to make her own way in the world. In fact, it was a challenge she appreciated. What she resented was how it had happened, so abruptly, even cruelly, without a thought to her feelings.

Saying that her family wasn't close was something of an understatement. Her family was selfish, all of them, including herself. They each cared more about their immediate world than each other, all of them including herself. Taylor hated that, and as her heels clicked across the bare floor, she yearned for it to be different. She yearned for more. She needed... something.

It wasn't often she allowed herself to need, but she needed to now. Sitting on her bed, she pulled out her cell phone and called Suzanne.

"How's my unit coming?" Suzanne asked. "Nearly ready for me?"

Taylor could hear pots and pans clattering, and smiled, feeling soothed already. For as long as she'd known Suzanne, she'd smelled like vanilla, had some sort of food stain on one part of her person or another and was always in the middle of whipping up something mouthwatering.

"Your unit is coming along," Taylor assured her. "You'll be opening Earthly Delights in no time."

"I'm ready."

"Me, too." Hopefully she'd be right next door opening her own store as well. If she could afford to get away without a tenant's monthly cash flow. She sighed. "I can't wait to have you around again."

The clanging slowed. "I thought you were enjoying your solitude."

"Yeah, well, not as much as I thought I would, it turns out."

Now the clanging stopped all together. "Taylor? What's the matter?"

Damn it, she'd given herself away. Caring deeply for her friends and opening up to them were two different things entirely, at least for her. She didn't open up easily.

Correction: she opened up never.

But complicating the matter was the simple fact that she didn't really even know what was wrong, she only knew she felt this unsettling and vague...need. For what exactly, she had no idea. "I just wanted to say hi."

"You sound...sad," Suzanne accused.

"I do not."

"Never mind. I'm coming over right after I finish up here. I won't be but another half hour. I'll bring ice cream, and you can tell me everything."

Ice cream happened to be Suzanne's cure-all for anything and everything. It usually worked, but this seemed bigger than even ice cream. "Chocolate?" Taylor asked pathetically. "Double fudge chocolate?"

"Chocolate," Suzanne promised. "Give me thirty minutes, hon, tops."

Tempting, oh God, it was so tempting. But no matter how much she loved Suzanne, Taylor had never been able to tell her about her own painful past, about her distant family, about losing Jeff, and somehow she knew that what she was feeling now was all tied up with that. And she couldn't go into it, not now, not after so many years of burying it, because she was afraid that if she did, if she let it out, it would destroy her all over again. "I have a Historical Society meeting this evening." True enough. "But maybe tomorrow, okay?"

"Promise?"

"Promise. Kiss Ryan for me."

"I wish you'd come stay with us so you could get away from the renovation, at least at night."

"I'm fine."

"I just don't like you there in the heart of downtown, all by yourself in that big old empty building."

"No one is going to bother me *because* the place is so old and empty. Don't worry about me, I'm safe."

"Of course I'll worry, but that won't stop you from doing as you please. Talk to you tomorrow?"

"Absolutely."

Taylor flipped off the cell phone, and had just slipped it back into her pocket when Mac spoke in that low, husky voice of his, nearly causing her to leap right out of her skin. "You didn't move out."

Damn. "Well aren't you observant." Slowly, on her own terms, she shifted on the bed to face him.

Big mistake.

First, sitting on the bed while he was standing right next to it made her feel a little bit shameless, a little bit...hungry.

Horrifyingly so.

And second, there was the way he was looking back at her—eyes heated, glinting with that edgy, unreadable expression that made her thighs tighten.

Did he wonder how combustive they'd be in this bed, the way she wondered? Not that she intended to follow through on that wondering, but...

"I don't know who you were just talking to," he said. "But they were right. It's not safe here at night, no matter what you think."

"Of course it is."

"The building is deserted, and in obvious renovation. You know damn well this street gets heavy foot traffic on a daily basis. You never know who's going to come pawing through here looking to steal supplies or tools."

"I lock up."

He let a rough snort.

"I'm staying, Mac."

"There are going to be times where there's no electricity. No water. No gas. This isn't going to be the Ritz, Princess. This is going to be little more than camping at best."

She hadn't had luxuries in months, but hell if she'd admit that. Or the fact that she was slowly selling off her beloved antique collection just to keep afloat here. He thought her a spoiled princess, so be it. What he thought was no skin off her nose.

And if he really believed she was going to back off the first challenge in her entire life, the first chance she'd ever had to prove herself, to get by on her own, he was sorely mistaken. She'd continue her spaghetti and canned tomato diet for as long as it took. She was going to do this, and do it right, and not even for him, the first man to make her feel a twinge in the heart region in ten years, would she give it up.

"I'll make sure I have batteries and drinking water," she said.

He stared at her for one, long, unwavering heartbeat, then shook his head. "Are you always impossible and stubborn, or is it just me?"

Trick question, that.

He certainly hadn't been the first man to find her difficult, and she doubted he'd be the last. But only one thing mattered to her, her battered pride. No way was she going to admit she couldn't afford to go anywhere for the duration of the renovation, not to him, not to anyone. "I'm staying, Mac."

"Through the dirt and noise, through the inconvenience, through the danger?"

The only possible danger came from him and him alone, but she doubted he'd appreciate the irony. "Through the dirt and noise, through the inconvenience, through the 'danger.'"

"Taylor—"

"Wow, my name," she marveled, cocking her head. "You *do* know it."

His jaw tightened. "You're doing this, aren't you? No matter what I say."

"I'm doing this." She had no choice. "No matter what you say."

4

SOUTH VILLAGE'S NIGHTLIFE rivaled the Sunset Strip as the busiest, most energetic area in Southern California. And yet the crowds it attracted weren't wild or aggressive. Instead the attitude was a sort of laid-back and easygoing elegance.

The town's founders had perpetrated this atmosphere with one goal in mind.

Wealth.

The old adage turned out to be correct—build it and they will come. The place had roared in the twenties, declined in the thirties and forties and rebelled in the fifties and sixties. True to the circle of life, it had been given a face-lift, slowly over the past twenty years, and had been turned into a gold mine.

As a result, there was never an available parking spot. Swearing, Mac circled the block. Then again. *Damn it*, he'd had a long day, all he needed was one little spot. Somewhere. Anywhere.

The heat was going to kill him. If Taylor didn't kill him first, that is. She could do it with just her eyes, those amazing green eyes she thought hid everything from to the world and yet seemed so expressive to him.

Then there was her calm and cool, sophisticated, elegant exterior, which he hated. But he also was beginning to understand all that was really just a front for a boiling pot of stubborn orneriness, and where there was stubborn orneriness, there was heat and passion.

And damn if he wasn't a sucker for heat and passion. Oh yeah, he enjoyed a woman who knew what she wanted and how.

Or at least, he used to.

But his and Taylor's fate was sealed, no matter how explosive he figured they'd be in bed, because she was everything he would never go for again.

And she was hiding something, he knew it. Something more than living in the building when he'd told her not to. God help her if it had something to do with this job, which he was depending on far too much for his own comfort.

Damn, letting himself feel again was a bitch.

And what he felt right now was hungry and tired, but attending tonight's monthly Historical Society meeting was necessary. Rubbing elbows with the powers that be made him want to grate his back teeth into powder, but it had to be done, because though no one would ever admit to it, it truly wasn't *what* you knew, but *who* you knew.

He needed to mingle.

Much to his perpetual disgust, the meetings were always run more like a cocktail party than the gathering and exchange of information they were supposed to be.

He hated cocktail parties.

The "meetings" were held at city hall, a building that could trace its roots to 1876, when it had been built as a grand hotel. In its day, it had housed miners, western settlers and Spanish royalty. Tonight the Spanish-style building was decorated in gold and silver, with froufrou food on platters that made him wish for a beer and a sloppy piece of pizza, New York style. The music came from a live quartet of musicians who didn't understand that being able to talk was important.

But at least air-conditioning blasted through the place. Early summer in Southern California hadn't disappointed, the temperature was in the nineties, the humidity off the scale.

In spite of the heat, anyone who was anyone in South Village was already there, schmoozing away. He counted three city councillors, the commissioner and the mayor before he worked his way past the entry hall.

There was a good reason for the crowd. Besides official business, and South Village did take its official business very seriously, the meeting's *true* underlying purpose was as a meat market.

The *single* meat market.

His mouth twisting cynically, he looked around. Oh yeah, singles galore, mostly hungry-looking socialites, circling the crowd, checking out the potential fixer-uppers—meaning the men they could live with, the men they could make putty in their well-manicured hands, the men whose names and expensive bank accounts they could take and be set for life.

Mac should know. After all, it had been a meeting just like this one when he was doing a little contracting on the side where his ex had scoped him out. She'd decided his last name was synonymous with money, and without bothering to figure out that Mac lived his own life as he damn well pleased *despite* his family's money, Ariel had gone after him with dollar signs in her eyes.

He was still ashamed to admit she'd caught him with little more than a toss of her perfect hair, a come-do-me smile and a crook of her red-tipped pinkie finger.

Damn memories.

Beating them back, he pasted a smile on his face and moved forward, determined to make nice and be seen.

AN HOUR LATER, Mac figured he'd done his job. He'd nodded, talked, even smiled with the board members he knew mattered most—Mayor Isabel W. Craftsman, known as a ruthlessly tough bitch, but widely tolerated because she'd done the city better than any mayor in history, Councilman Daniel Oberman, a man who used to be a builder, and was known for his genuine love of the renovation projects.

And so many others his head spun.

Not only spun, but pounded. It was little wonder, when he considered the hours he'd put in this week, and now that he'd bared his teeth into a smile and played nice, he was out of here.

Or would have been, except that he saw her. Taylor Wellington, current bane of his existence.

She wore a haltered shimmery dress that came to midthigh in the exact color of a summer sky. Her legs were bare and tanned, and longer than the legal limit. She stood surrounded by a group of women who also looked as if maybe they made a career out of looking spiffed up and polished. Each of them could have graced any cover of a glossy magazine, and yet to Mac they all looked plastic.

Taylor, too. He wanted her to be plastic. He really wanted that.

Then she looked up, her eyes unerringly finding his. And in a flash that came so quick he figured he had to be seeing things, she shifted from cool as a cucumber to hot as a wildfire.

His heart clutched. It wasn't a pleasant sort of clutch either, but the kind that took hold and squeezed.

What was she doing, looking at him like that?

Her gaze stayed locked on his, despite the fact that people were talking to her, despite the fact there were people smiling and nodding at him as they passed. The music, the hum of conversation, everything, seemed to fade away.

Then she controlled that flash of heat, smoothing her expression as if it'd never happened, leaving her cool as rain. She had a real talent for that, for hiding her thoughts.

Good, he decided. He didn't want to know them.

But she kept looking, every bit as much as he was, and as if he was attached by a bungee cord to her eyes, her body, he started moving toward her, away from the front door he'd been so eager to get out only a moment ago.

She watched him come.

And when he was close, his other senses came

back. He could feel the cool air, could hear the sculptured, glamorous redhead on her left say, "I'm surprised to see you here tonight, Taylor. We'd actually heard you'd...how should I put it? That you'd come down on the social ladder a bit."

"All the way down," said the perfectly groomed country club woman on her right. "Like to the bottom rung."

Several of the other women laughed, the kind of laugh that assures everyone you're only laughing *with* the person at the butt of the joke, but was really a crock because there was no doubt.

They were laughing *at* Taylor.

She broke eye contact with Mac to stare at them, her eyes distant and assessing as if she felt far above such mockery.

"We heard about the will," Country Club Chick said, making an effort to look solemn instead of cruelly gleeful, and failing miserably. "Did your grandfather really cut you off without a cent and give everything to your mother?"

Taylor gave her a long stare. "What does it matter? I don't need anyone's money."

As if she'd told a great joke, they all burst out into collective laughter.

Taylor simply tightened her glossy mouth.

"You're so funny," the redhead said. "You always make me laugh."

"Your mother looks good," Country Club Chick number two said, looking out into the crowd at someone Mac couldn't see. "No doubt she's guaranteed a successful campaign for the next election with all her daddy's money."

"No doubt," Taylor said.

Mac didn't know what the hell they were talking about, but as he hadn't taken his eyes off Taylor, he saw something that shocked him.

Though it didn't show in her casual stance, he saw it in her eyes. She was letting them get to her. She cared what these women thought. She cared a lot.

Oh, man. He should have run out the front door and never looked back. Why hadn't he done that?

Another of the Sorority Bunch patted Taylor's arm. "Well, I for one think it's very brave of you to keep your chin up."

"And at least you still have all your amazing clothes." This from the redhead, who was eyeing Taylor's gorgeous dress. "You can just learn to repeat wear."

"Hey, and don't worry, we'll pick up your tab on our monthly lunches," offered yet another.

Mac's fingers itched to wrap themselves around a few necks. The urge made no sense, as only a few moments ago he'd have sworn Taylor fit perfectly into this not so cozy little circle.

But suddenly she didn't look plastic like the others, she looked...real.

And, damn it to hell, she also looked hurt.

"Really, it's touching how concerned you are about my financial affairs," she said in a voice dripping with chill. "Truly touching."

No one but Mac grinned.

"But don't worry about me. I'm going to be just fine." She turned and walked away, away from the women, away from him.

Head high, she avoided any more conversation by striding with direct purpose to the veranda doors, which led to the botanical gardens kept by the Historical Society.

She walked right out the doors and into the night. And like a puppy needing a belly rub, he followed.

5

TAYLOR DREW A DEEP BREATH as she stepped into the hot, hot summer night, refusing to react. If she remained numb, then she wouldn't feel her burning throat and eyes, or the ache in her chest. If she remained numb, she wouldn't feel the fist around her heart, squeezing, squeezing.

It wasn't just the pettiness that upset her, or that she'd thought of those women as friends.

She didn't care about them. She didn't care what they thought.

It simply all came back to that *alone* thing. And she felt so damn alone. Ironic, when she considered her own mother had been inside the party. Oh, they'd kissed hello, air kisses of course, not daring to wrinkle their clothes with a hug. They'd smiled and had made light conversation.

How are you?

Fine, thanks.

Oh, good. You look great.

Surface stuff that meant nothing.

The night was hot, the air thick with the humidity

that hadn't faded from the heat of the day, but that was good. She needed the warmth after the chill of the past hour.

The noises of the party followed her onto the veranda as she walked to the railing and looked down onto the gardens that were considered the most beautiful in all of South Village.

They were stunning, lovingly tended to by generous Historic Society volunteers. Volunteers not afraid of getting their hands dirty or their silk wrinkled.

Which meant a Wellington had never gotten on their knees and so much as pulled a weed in those gardens, including Taylor. Oh sure, she'd volunteered in other ways, by attending expensive charity functions and writing big, fat checks backed by her grandfather.

What kind of woman did that, got to the age of twenty-seven completely supported by someone else's money? She deserved the pity she'd gotten from those women tonight, but not for the reasons they thought.

She'd never actually worked hard at anything.

Until now.

Leaning on the railing, she rubbed her temples, shedding her tough shell and half her makeup by swiping beneath her damp eyes. Poor little rich girl, she thought with loathing for the moment of self-pity.

Ex-rich girl.

Was it so odd that she'd wanted something from her own mother tonight, after all this time? A real hug? A real smile? Even a real touch? She shouldn't have bothered coming, should have stayed home.

At the thought of what awaited her there, an empty building stripped down to the studs and a stack of bills so high it made her head spin, her eyes filled again.

God, she felt so alone. So damn alone.

"Taylor."

At the low, gruff voice she was beginning to know all too well, she stilled. He had a terrible habit of coming up on her in the most vulnerable of moments. "Go away."

"Yeah, about that."

She heard his footsteps. Coming closer, damn him. "Mac—"

"You'd like me to vanish, I know. And believe me, I'd like that, too.

In direct opposition to those words, he came even closer. Then closer still, until he set a lean hip against the railing, facing her, his chest brushing her shoulder as he stared down at her while she did her best impression of someone desperately interested in the flowers.

"I wanted to leave before I even got here," he said.

"So what's holding you?" She wouldn't look at him, couldn't. No one saw her vulnerable and lived. She didn't care how big he was, how warm— Oh God, he was warm. Heat radiated off him, and despite the hot, sticky night, she wanted more of it.

The need alone made her eyes sting all over again, and released a few of the tears she couldn't blink back. And then, because she'd been holding her breath, she gave herself away with one horrifyingly obvious sniff.

"Ah, hell," he muttered. His big hands settled on her bare upper arms as he turned her to face him, and for the life of her, she couldn't look away. "What's going on?" he asked.

What was going on? Only everything.

"Princess?"

Suddenly his pet name for her didn't seem like an insult, not when uttered in the husky, slightly rough voice that was far softer than she imagined he could ever be. Unable to talk without making a bigger fool of herself, she just shook her head.

With the rough pad of his thumb, he stroked a tear off her cheek. She hadn't worn waterproof mascara, so she probably looked like a raccoon, but even more worrisome than that was the way she reacted to his touch. His thumb continued to make lazy passes over her cheek, his other fingers sank into her hair, and she stood there fighting the most insidious need to sob her heart out.

Silent and strong, he waited, not rushing her, not freaking out because she was crying, not doing anything but waiting patiently for her to pull herself together.

And suddenly she didn't want to pull herself together, she wanted to bury her face against his shoulder and let go. It was humiliating, appalling, and as if he could read her mind, he made a low, soft sound of empathy in his throat that completely undid her.

"Everything they said was true," she whispered. "I grew up a spoiled brat." She waited for some sort of recrimination but he said nothing.

His fingers on her temple were the most soothing touches she'd ever felt. And maybe because of it, or maybe because it was the dark, her mouth ran away with her good sense and she spilled it all. "My family...we're not close. I don't know why really, we're just...different from one another I guess."

"Not every family is super tight."

"We're not even in the realm of tight. Growing up, I was given the fanciest education. On Grandfather's money. Every few years or so he'd come around and see how his investment was doing, but other than that, we didn't have much contact. I always thought it was because I disappointed him somehow. Or that he just didn't have much sentiment in him, but he seemed to enjoy my sisters' company."

"Taylor—"

"No." Not wanting his pity, please God, not his pity, she didn't look at him. "You know what? Just forget it."

"You started it, finish it."

It was amazing how private the veranda was for how many people were just inside. Maybe nobody but the two of them dared the evening heat and humidity.

Mac didn't mention it one way or another, he seemed focused on her, and only her, and having that much man, all tall, gorgeous and listening to her, really listening, was...well, a fairly intense experience. "My grandfather died," she said to the night. "And the will was rather...interesting."

"How interesting?"

"Well, for one thing, he left me the building you're working on."

"It's a beauty."

"Oh yes," she agreed. "And a money pit."

He nodded.

"He...took away the funds that had always been

available to me. Every penny. Gave it all to my mother knowing she'd never share." She closed her eyes and admitted the last painful truth. "Leaving me flat broke."

"Why wouldn't your mother share?"

"She's been saving for a rainy day all her life, she's...frugal." She let out a harsh laugh. "The richest frugal person you'll ever meet."

"What about your dad?"

"He's remarried. Lives in Europe, and I don't see him very often."

"They were talking about your mother as if she were there tonight."

"She was," she said. "She's Isabel Craftsman."

Mac's eyes widened. "The mayor?"

"The one and only."

"So you're one of *those* Wellingtons."

"That would be me. One of *those* Wellingtons." It usually went one of two ways from here. Either the person would stare at her in awe, because her mother, cold and precise as she was, had done excellent things for the city, or the person would sneer, because let's face it, her mother hadn't gotten to where she was by making friends.

But Mac looked neither awed nor disgusted. "You really can't go to her if you need help?"

"I could, but..."

"You won't," he finished for her, his eyes filling with something she hadn't seen from him before. Respect. "What about your sisters?"

"Like I said, we're not that close."

"The building is worth a fortune."

"If I sold it." She opened her eyes and with fierce determination said, "Which I'm not doing. I'm not walking away from this. I'm not like them, Mac, those women in there, I'm not going to be like them if it kills me."

"You're not anything like them," he agreed.

She'd wanted someone on her side tonight, she'd wanted blind comfort, and this man, her virtual opposite, the thorn in her side, was offering it.

No one had done such a thing for her since Jeff.

Just the thought of him now, with Mac right there, felt like a betrayal to his memory, a stab to her already wounded heart, but Mac was throwing her, reacting the way she'd expect Suzanne to react. A friend. A girlfriend.

Not a man.

But she didn't need him to react this way. She'd learned to depend on no one but herself. She was all she needed, she'd always simply comforted herself, and—

Mac continued to stand there when she sniffed

again, not running, not reacting to her tears with his own reasoning.

He simply opened his arms.

And she stepped right into them. Stepped into them and steeped herself in his giving heat and over-whelming strength. Then she did as she'd wanted to, she buried her face in the crook of his neck, deeply inhaling the scent of wood, soap and one-hundred-percent man.

Sinking his fingers into her hair, he lifted her face so he could look into it. She looked back, at the chiseled angle of his jaw, his slightly curved lips, his light golden eyes as they ran over her face before locking on hers.

Taylor felt the jolt of his gaze all the way to her toes. She didn't know how it was possible, but in his arms her problems seemed to fade away, chased by equal parts awareness and a morbid excitement she couldn't, wouldn't, deny. Winding her arms around his neck, she pressed a little closer, absorbing the helpless growl of awareness that rumbled up from Mac's chest.

A matching awareness combined with a heady female power that sizzled through her, because he felt it, too, whether he wanted to or not, he felt it, too. Proving it, his hands tightened on her, skimmed down her back, then slowly back up again, chasing any lingering chill with a blooming desire she hadn't expected or wanted but wouldn't deny. "Um...this might be a good time for you to tell me you're married," she said. "Or something."

"I'm not married." His mouth quirked. "Or something. I'm not anything with anyone."

Chest to breast, belly to belly, she stared at him, and he stared at her right back. In that moment, he was the only person in her entire world. Her body felt overwhelmed by that, even as she leaned into him.

Around them, the air crackled, growing more intense by the second in the hot, summer night, until she could hardly breathe. "Mac..."

"Yeah?"

She sighed.

"Taylor? What is it?"

"I want..." *You*, she thought. *I want you*.

Obeying the rampant need and invitation in her breathy voice, he bent his head and kissed her. Softly at first, but then she wrapped her arms around his neck, tight, so that the next kiss came hard, a rapacious, devouring kiss that was wildly carnal and full of erotic intent, and couldn't have been more deeply intimate if they'd been entirely alone in the world.

"Is that what you were looking for?" he asked

when he pulled back, his voice even rougher than usual.

"Yes." Taylor was breathing hard, and was slightly gratified to see he was, too. For a long moment they just stared at each other, with Taylor's brain not fully functioning because he'd just destroyed her with yet another devastating thought—she hadn't lost herself in a man like that since...*since*.

She hadn't wanted to.

She would have backed away then, and might even have started running, but his hands were still on her, still holding her securely against him. And in fact, hers were still curled around his neck, her body glued to his.

Of its own free will.

His eyes, locked on hers, were scorching, his body against hers rock hard, obviously aroused, obviously hungry for more. And yet he stood there, waiting.

Who would have expected patience from a man like Mac?

She could take him home. They could spend an energetic, adventurous evening exhausting each other. It would be hot and fast and good. But...and she couldn't believe this, but...it wouldn't be enough. For the first time since Jeff, casual sex wouldn't be enough, not even with Mac.

"I'm going home now," she said softly, and touched his granite jaw. "Alone."

"Yeah." Turning his head, he kissed her palm. "I know."

Not sure whether she was relieved or insulted—wasn't he even going to try to talk his way into her bed?—she backed out of his arms.

What did she do now, thank him? The thought made her want to let out a laugh, but it would have been a slightly hysterical one, so she put her fingers to her mouth and swallowed hard. "I'm...I'm thinking that kiss might have been a bad idea."

"Yeah."

Now she did laugh. "You might have at least argued."

"Taylor...was that a normal kind of kiss to you?"

Since her lips still tingled and her heart still pounded, she shook her head.

"No," he agreed. "And that kind of connection is nothing to mess with."

"You've been hurt, too," she said quietly, surprised, and mad at herself for not seeing it sooner.

He opened his mouth, then closed it again. Then sighed. "I was married. A long time ago."

"Do you...have kids?"

A spasm of pain crossed his face. "No. It didn't

work out. It didn't work out so much that I never intend to get serious again."

"Never?"

"Never. Ever. Do you follow me?"

"I follow you. I even agree with you." Her lips quirked in a mirthless smile. "Imagine that."

Then, with her body still humming with desire, she took a step away. "Good night, Mac."

"Good night, Taylor."

MAC WATCHED HER saunter off, cool as rain, head high, and let out a slow, shaky breath. Holy shit, that had been some kiss.

Kisses.

He took a careful, long wobbly breath to even be able to see straight. Another to relax his entire body, which was quite…tense now, thanks to Taylor's hot, long, sleek bod that she'd plastered to his.

He'd lost himself in her, totally lost himself, when he'd promised himself he'd never do that again.

Well, he was going to have to be more careful than that next time she flashed those expressive, hurting eyes, wasn't he?

Much more careful.

6

TAYLOR WAS GRATEFUL to have the entire weekend looming in front of her before the work of reframing and rewindowing began in earnest. Two days of no construction. No pounding, no people, no decisions to make, nothing.

And no Mac.

Two days in which to do as she pleased, which would include no thinking, no obsessing and no wasted regrets on what had happened between them on a dark night in the amazing gardens at the town hall.

On what *hadn't* happened, and why.

Being a logical thinker most of the time—though that logic had deserted her in Mac's arms—she had a stack of reasons. He was just too...strong. Strong-minded, strong-willed, strong everything. A good part of that strength came from a superb control.

But *Taylor* wanted to be the one in control. She liked that, a lot. When she chose to let a man in, she wanted to run the show.

She doubted anyone ran Mac's show.

Then there was the fact that he'd seen her at her weakest. No one ever saw her weak and lived to tell the tale, so she figured she'd lay low for the rest of the time they had to be near each other.

Problem solved.

It was only...at least two more months. Damn, that was a long time.

He'd loved his wife. Loved her so much he couldn't bear to ever love again. Funny how that gave her heart a hard tug, even though she'd sworn the same thing about herself after she'd lost Jeff. Still swore that same thing.

That such a big, fierce, independent man could be laid so low by such emotion that she understood so much...well, she was quite certain that shouldn't make her want him all the more.

The sudden pounding on the front door of the building, which she'd locked, made her jump. It was a Saturday, an early Saturday. There was no reason for anyone to be here, so it was with a frown for her solitude that she went out of her apartment, down the stairs to the front door of the building, and looked out the peep hole.

Nicole and Suzanne stood on the other side holding up a tub of ice cream, three spoons and matching ear-to-ear grins.

With more joy than Taylor had felt all week she

yanked the door open. "You guys read my mind." She reached for the ice cream but Nicole held her off.

"Not so fast." She eyed Taylor carefully. "Yep, you were right," she said to Suzanne. "Something's wrong."

Now they both stared at Taylor, and she squirmed. "Don't be silly, I'm fine."

But despite the claim, she was immediately enveloped in a bear hug that brought tears to her eyes.

Again.

"Oh, honey." The lush, redheaded Suzanne pulled back, handed Nicole the spoons and held Taylor's face in her hands. "What is it?"

What, did the woman have radar? Taylor patted her hair, her clothes, but everything was in place. Everything was always in place. Her own little armor.

"Yeah, you look gorgeous as ever," Nicole said in disgust. Nicole was an emergency room doctor who considered fashion and hairstyling a grievous waste of time. She was beautiful in spite of it. Now she looked Taylor over with that X-ray vision all doctors seemed to possess. "And let me tell you, it's disgusting how good you can look surrounded by drywall dust and destruction. Now spill it. What's the matter?"

"Nothing." Taylor forced a smile. "Allergies, that's all."

"Bullshit." Nicole led the way up the stairs, back into Taylor's apartment, where they all sat on the bed and took a spoon. "Let's hear it. Long version please."

Taylor dug into the double fudge chocolate, consuming a bazillion calories in one bite. "I told you, I'm fine."

"You know, you never let Suzanne or I get away with telling you we're fine when we're not, so don't give it to us." Nicole waved her spoon. "Now. Who's the asshole who put that look of misery on your pretty face?"

"There's no—" She looked into their expectant, worried expressions and let out a slow, shaky breath. For courage she inhaled another hundred calories, maybe two hundred. "Mac. His name is Mac. He's my contractor."

"And?" Nicole lifted a brow. "I definitely hear an 'and' at the end of that sentence."

"And…" What the hell. "He kisses like heaven."

Suzanne sucked on her spoon and smiled. "Ah."

"Ah what?" Taylor demanded.

"You're falling for him."

"Because I think he kisses like heaven?"

"Because you have stars in your eyes when you say it," Suzanne said gently. "You're falling hard, sweetie."

"Lust or love?" Nicole wanted clarified in her usual blunt way.

"*Lust,*" Taylor said.

Nicole cocked her head. "You said that way too quickly."

"I'm staying single, Nicole. No question."

Suzanne reached for Taylor's hand. "Tell us why love is such a bad thing. Who hurt you?"

"Life," Taylor said simply. She was not going into that now. Maybe not ever. "Look, I've tried love. It hurts, all right?"

"Not always," Nicole and Suzanne said at the same time.

But Taylor wasn't interested. Wouldn't ever be interested.

ON MONDAY MORNING Mac made sure the framing and window replacement was going smoothly, then sought out Taylor.

He found her sitting on her bed, and was utterly unprepared for how just the sight of her felt like a punch in the gut, and for how much he wanted to haul her up and back into his arms.

He'd figured he'd gotten her out of his system Friday night. Way out.

Apparently, he'd figured wrong.

She was looking more put together than anyone had any business looking at seven o'clock in the morning. Her shiny blond hair fell loose to her shoulders, perfectly combed. She wore pale yellow trousers with a matching sleeveless top that screamed class. The top dipped down in front and back, just enough to give him a peek of creamy skin and curves, and make him need a drink of water for his suddenly parched throat. Her long, long legs were crossed, a sandal dangling off her big toe as she lightly swung her foot while she talked into her cell phone with those perfectly glossed lips.

She saw him immediately, and though she didn't so much as smile at him, the awareness in the room bounced off the walls.

She was talking to someone about the sale of an antique wine rack, her voice even and firm as she discussed money with a single-mindedness he figured he understood a lot better today than he had last week.

The woman could drive a hard bargain, and in spite of himself, he watched in awe as she wheedled what sounded like a mind-boggling price for her piece.

When she hung up the phone, her eyes were sparkling with triumph and...relief.

Which brought him to the reason he stood there. "Good morning," he said.

"Morning." She was all business—and avoiding his gaze. "You've got a crew here already, I can hear them. I'll just get out of your hair." She slipped her foot back into her sandal.

"I'd like to talk to you."

"I'm...uh..." She looked around, probably for a handy excuse.

"Save it, Princess. You want to ignore me on a personal level after one kiss, fine."

He had to give her credit, she didn't so much as sputter. "I'd already forgotten about that 'one kiss,'" she said evenly.

"Really?"

She let out a long breath. "No."

Just like that, his heart tweaked, good and hard. "If it's any consolation, you've pretty much kept me up all night for the past two nights running," he admitted.

She lifted a shoulder as if she didn't care, but her eyes warmed a little. "It's some consolation, I suppose."

"Look, Taylor..."

"I don't think talking about it is the right thing to do. Under the circumstances."

"Circumstances?"

"That we're not going to let it happen again," she said.

"Right." But it bugged him that he knew why *he* didn't want it to happen again, but not why *she* didn't. "Look, I get it now, why you didn't move out.

You have nowhere else to go, no money, and you're stuck here until we're done."

"Well, why don't you just spell it out," she said with a mirthless little laugh.

"This isn't about your pride, Taylor. Bottom line, you're putting every cent into this building and don't want to waste it on paying for a place to live."

She lifted her hands. "Caught me."

Stepping closer, he watched her pupils dilate a little.

Because of their closeness? It was affecting him, too, he could smell her, some exotic combination of sweet and sexy, and he could see the pulse at the base of her neck beating wildly, a dead giveaway that she was not as calm as she wanted to be. "I'm trying to tell you we'll work around you," he said. "We'll do this room last."

"But you said you wanted to hit it all at once, so that you didn't have to get your subcontractors back through here again. You said that it was hard enough to—"

"I know what I said. I'm telling you I'll make the adjustments."

"Why?"

"Does it matter?"

"To me, yes."

"Because as my client, I want you to be happy with the job."

"As your client," she repeated, sounding a little...hurt?

Impossible.

"I'm just trying to do the right thing here," he said.

"Because you feel sorry for me?"

"Hell, no. You're too ornery to feel sorry for."

For a long moment she just stared at him, then a ghost of a smile curved those lush lips. "Okay, then. As long as it's not that. Oh, and Mac?" She climbed off the bed with the smooth grace of a sleek cat, no longer looking plastic. She would never look plastic to him again, and as she came close, he actually had to fist his hands to keep them off her.

"Thank you," she said softly.

He didn't want to contemplate what just that smile of hers did to his insides. Did she know? Probably not, or she wouldn't still be looking at him like that. They'd both agreed—nothing could, or would, happen. But he had to make sure. "Now, about the personal stuff."

Her face closed up again and he had to laugh. "After all you're going through, I'd think a little kiss would be the least of your problems."

"If it had been just one 'little kiss,'" she said, shocking him with her boldness, "then it *would* be the least of my problems."

Hell. At her sides, her own hands were fisted. Because she couldn't keep her hands off him either, or because she wanted to slug him? "Tell me why you don't want this," he asked quietly.

"Truth?"

"Truth."

She lifted her head, so close to him now that they could have leaned in just a fraction and had their mouths meet. "I do casual," she whispered. "I do casual real well. But not more than that, not ever more. And this..." She sighed, closed her eyes. "This feels like more to me, Mac, and it scares me to death."

"Yeah. Look, I—"

"Mac." One of his laborers stood in the doorway. "You're needed downstairs."

Taylor turned away.

"We'll finish this later," he told her slim back.

She lifted a shoulder.

"Taylor—"

"I don't think that's necessary."

"Oh, it's necessary," he said, watching her stiffen. He was sorry for that, but they worked together, would have to continue to do so.

They had to finish talking about this, they had to.

Then maybe he could stop thinking about it.

7

BUT LATER NEVER CAME. Not that day and not the next, because Taylor did something Mac didn't expect. She avoided him. She avoided him good.

She avoided him through the installation of all the plumbing and electrical. Through the hanging and taping of the new drywall.

Which admittedly wasn't that difficult, as he used good subcontractors, and for nearly two weeks his presence wasn't required more than an hour here and there.

One morning he stood out front of her building with the hose, spraying down the tools they'd used to texture the new walls, lost in concentration, when a breathy female voice whispered "excuse me" in his ear.

Head whipping up, his gaze collided with...*a petite version of Taylor?* He'd have sworn Taylor Wellington was a serious one-of-a-kind, yet this woman had the blond hair, the same see-through green eyes, the matching cynical tilt to her head...but that's where the similarities ended.

She came barely to his shoulders, and where Taylor defined elegance and sophistication, this slightly younger version defined urban hip. She was dressed in painted on jeans and a little crop top that showed off a sparkling diamond in her belly button, and when she turned around in a circle with a little delighted laugh, he saw the rose tattoo rising above her belt line.

Now, why anyone would want a plant growing out of their butt boggled the mind, but having passed his thirtieth birthday almost two years ago, he'd discovered he was completely out of touch when it came to such things.

"I look a lot like her, don't I?" She grinned. "I'm Liza. Taylor's baby sister. And you're…"

"Mac."

"The current boy toy?"

She actually batted her lashes as she asked this, and suddenly Mac saw another difference. Where Taylor's eyes and voice were soft at times, even giving, there was nothing soft about Liza. She was cold and hard, and had been around the block more than once. "Boy toy?" he repeated, scratching his jaw. "Uh…no."

Liza laughed. "You're rougher than her usual type, which is usually way too…upscale for me." A sideways look raked over his body, slowly. "But if she put you in a well-tailored suit...oh yeah, baby, I can see her going for you." Running her tongue over her bottom lip, she looked at him from beneath half-closed, sleepy, sexy eyes. "You're hot."

It'd been awhile since a woman had come on to him so blatantly. In fact, he nearly looked behind him to make sure she was talking to him.

"I have to give it to good old sis," Liza said. "She always did have great taste. Some advice though, just don't get attached. Taylor doesn't dabble with one man for long, not since Jeff."

"Jeff?"

"Her one great love," she said with overplayed dramatic flair, and stepping close, she ran a finger over his shoulder, down his arm. "Sis is under the mistaken impression that he was the greatest guy on the planet, and that her turn at happiness has come and gone. Stupid, huh? I mean there are billions of guys on this planet." Her eyes went sultry, speculative. "So how about it, big boy? Are you playing with Taylor, or are you available?"

He caught her wandering finger just as it roamed down his chest toward his navel. "I'm the contractor."

"Ah, the contractor." Her eyes darkened as she looked up at the building. "Grandpa always did like her best."

Mac figured the sisters weren't very close if even he knew better than that.

"So is she here?" She tossed her head, flipping her hair artfully around her face. "Or are we all alone?"

"Look..." He wracked his brain for her name. "Liza—"

"Uh-oh." She affected a pout, and before he could stop her, she cupped his face in her hands. "You're scowling. Didn't your momma ever tell you that would give you wrinkles?"

Now she rested her body against his, making sure to rub up against the vee of his jeans like a cat in heat. "Or maybe you don't care about wrinkles. Men never do, they don't need to. Your laugh lines are sexy."

Curling his fingers around her wrists, he pried her off him and held her away. "Okay, that's enough—"

"Liza!"

Liza didn't flinch at her sister's voice, just stuck out that lower lip even further as she turned to face Taylor, who came out of the building, looking sophisticated and elegant as ever, even with her eyes flashing.

"Hey, sis." Liza sidled back up to Mac. "Look what I found."

"Stop torturing my contractor."

"Oh, Taylor, but he's so gorgeous. Can I keep

him?" Mashing her breasts against Mac's arm, she batted her lashes at Taylor, who looked immune. "Pretty please?"

"Knock it off." She wore a loose and flowing white skirt, a bright red top and wide-brimmed straw hat. And looked good enough to eat.

Mac was suddenly starving. He separated himself from Liza, not an easy feat. Taylor was looking at him again, and he still didn't have a clue to what she was thinking.

"What do you need, Liza?" she asked her sister.

"You aren't going to even invite me in, show me around?"

"That's not why you're here."

Liza tried sticking her lower lip out further but Taylor didn't budge or soften her expression. "Money," Liza muttered. "I need money."

"Try asking your mother."

"She's your mother, too."

Taylor just stared at Liza, not giving an inch.

"Well, she's so damn tightfisted, what's the point?" Liza muttered.

Taylor lifted a brow, apparently agreeing with that assessment, but she shook her head. "I have nothing to give you."

"You never have anything to give."

Taylor closed her eyes briefly. "I'm sorry about the

times I wasn't there for you when I could have been. But the truth is, now that I might want to help, I can't. I just can't."

"Yeah, whatever. It's no skin off my nose." With one last lingering look at Mac, she spun on her heels and stalked off.

"Liza."

Liza didn't look back, just let herself out of the gate where she faded into the noon crowd on the streets.

Mac expected Taylor to spin on her heels as well, heading back into the building. Or toward her car. Instead, she just stood there, lost in her own world.

Eyeing her with wariness, he stepped closer. "Your sister is...interesting."

She lifted her head and looked at him. Her eyes were filled with annoyance, temper and a good amount of heat. "She's the baby of the family, and I'd say a spoiled rotten brat, but what she really is, is a woman-child desperate for attention."

"That was no child."

"No, you're right, she's twenty-one, old enough to know better. Did she...bother you before I got out here?"

"No."

"Did she...sexually harass you?"

Mac let out a bark of laughter at that. "Yeah. And I'm going to sue over my good honor."

"I'm serious, Mac."

"I'm going to live."

"Yes, but..." She looked at him. Looked at the sky. Then back at him. "Mac..."

A disparaging sound escaped her. "I'm trying to say I'm..."

Mac cocked his head, studying the uncomfortable Taylor with curiosity. "You're trying to say...what?"

"I just wanted to..." She held her breath, then let out a huff and turned in a slow circle while Mac waited.

Something was sticking in her craw, but what, he had no idea. Unless...oh yeah. She was trying to apologize. What was so interesting about that was that she looked as if she might choke over it. "Problem?" he asked, suddenly feeling like smiling.

"No. I just wanted to say..."

"Yes?"

"I'm *sorry.*" She glared at him as if this was all his fault. "I'm sorry if Liza came onto you and made you uncomfortable. I'm sorry you had to deal with her on the job. It was unfair and...and..."

"And you're sorry." He grinned now, because who would have known she could look adorable. "That was pretty tough, huh? Using the s-word?"

"It's even harder with you laughing at me," she said, adding a look of daggers.

"Oh, no, I'm not laughing at you, I'm laughing *with* you." But he kept on grinning, which pretty much made smoke come out her ears.

Her eyes were twin pools of fire. And her body language, hands fisted on her hips, shoulders back, head up... Battle ready, she was, no doubt.

Call him sick, but he liked it, he liked to see her temper flare, though he was quite certain he'd be risking certain death to admit such a thing to her. "I don't suppose you'd try to say it again, so I can watch you squirm some more?"

"You're a bastard, you know that?"

"Yep," he told her back as she stalked off. "I've definitely heard that one before."

Stopping, Taylor slowly turned back to face him. She'd barely been able to resist the urge to put her hands on her hips and stomp her feet like a child at the sight of Liza snuggled up to him, but that would be churlish, even childish.

And certainly she had amused him enough already.

But nobody laughed at her, nobody.

And yet there he stood, hair blowing in the breeze, eyes lit with good humor—at her expense—his long, lean, rangy body relaxed as can be.

That even now she could look at him and feel a

spark, feel a need to launch herself against him and hold on tight, really burned.

"Watch your pretty sandals there, Princess," he said, pointing to where she stood, which was next to his hose. The water had started to pool.

That it was still morning didn't matter in the summertime heat of Southern California. She hadn't even realized how hot she was until the chilled water lapped over her toes.

She eyed the hose. Eyed Mac.

"Don't even think about it," he said in a warning tone that cooked her goose all the way to finish.

"Oh, I'm thinking about it." She'd do more than think. Very carefully she set her hat down on the grass. She loved that hat and didn't want it to get wet like Mac was going to. He was going to get very wet.

"Taylor," he said in that low, gruff, thrillingly sexy voice.

But not only did no one laugh at her, no one told her what to do.

Ever.

Before she knew it, she'd picked up the hose and turned it on him, hitting him full in the chest.

The water was cold, which, she supposed, explained his yelp. Or it might have to do with the fact she lowered her aim just a bit.

The sound that escaped him now was a definite growl, a growl that signified an upcoming battle.

Half horrified, half exhilarated, she continued to hold the hose on him and stepped closer.

It knocked him back a step, and a group of people who'd come out of the ice-cream shop across the street whooped and hollered.

Mac ignored them, grinning a wholly evil grin at her that made her hesitate a moment.

Which is how he tackled her to the patch of grass behind her, holding her down with his big, warm, strong body sprawled over hers.

She couldn't believe it, but he'd gotten the best of her. Her, Taylor Wellington, a woman no one got the better of, ever.

Thankfully the wood fence across the front of her property, while mostly decoration, was high enough to now block them from view of pedestrian traffic, so she didn't have to think about that humiliation.

Lifting his face, Mac smiled a little wickedly down into hers, water raining off him onto her skin. Then he gathered her hands in one of his and yanked them above her head. One strong thigh insinuated its way between hers, pegging her between the soft, cool grass and the not even close to soft, definitely not cool body of Mac.

"Get off me," she hissed, wriggling, trying to free herself. "We're right out front, anyone could—"

"Could what? Could see this? *Good.*"

And eyes burning with intent, he dipped his head, covering her mouth with his.

8

TAYLOR GAVE one startled squeak, but then as sensations bombarded her—his hands on hers, his tongue sweeping into her mouth, his deliciously big, hard, wet body holding hers down, his powerful thigh holding hers open—she melted against him like lava. Her fingers curled against his, her body arching up to meld to every inch of his. And his mouth... Oh, his mouth.

She hadn't been able to think the first time they'd kissed, could barely think now, but he tasted like heaven. And now that she *was* thinking it, fully appreciating it, she realized something else. He knew just what to do with that mouth, knew how to nibble the corners of hers until she wanted to moan for more, knew to start out with little coaxing strokes of his tongue, then nip at her bottom lip with his teeth, soothing it over with a soft, sucking motion that whipped her into a desperate, impatient, wild thing, a wild thing with absolutely no shame, not to mention thoughts of rules or propriety.

Needing to put her hands on him, she flexed hers

beneath his, and he let her go. Oh yes, she thought, mindlessly arching up to him, running her now free hands over his wet shoulders, down his wet spine, oh yes, this is what she'd needed this morning when she'd woken up so inexplicably...sad.

This. Him. *Now.*

With a little sigh of pure unadulterated pleasure, she hugged him even closer, and wanting to give back as good as she was getting, she sucked his tongue into her mouth.

She was rewarded by a ragged groan ripped from deep in his chest, and felt his hands slip beneath her, cupping her bottom in his hands so that he could more fully seat himself between her thighs. At the feel of his erection, she whimpered in helpless delight, and squirmed, trying to get more of it.

Then he slowly lifted his head, her lips clinging as they parted because she didn't want it to end.

"Taylor." His voice was satisfactorily thick. Raspy. And looking down into her pouting face, he let out a soft sound of desire and stroked her jaw. "God, you're beautiful."

The grass beneath her was cool, and damp. Above them the sun was warm and dry, chasing the chill away from their wet clothes. But now, without Mac's mouth on hers, she could think again. Thoughts like her mascara was probably smeared, and that he'd eaten off all her gloss. That she was wrinkling, and probably staining one of her favorite skirts.

Or that she lay on her back, legs spread, heart wide open and vulnerable, to a man.

It was that last that made her close her eyes.

With a sigh, Mac rolled off her. On his back, staring up at the sky, he reached for her hand.

"What was that?" she whispered, eyes still closed, her breathing not even close to normal. But she let him entwine his fingers with hers, and gripped them back. "What the hell was that?"

"Whatever it was, it was damn good."

"Yeah." Turning her head, she found him studying the clouds floating overhead.

"There's Bambi," he said, and with his free hand pointed to a cloud.

Taylor had to laugh. "Bambi?"

"Yeah. There. And see that one? That long, sleek one to the right? A sailboat."

"Mmm." She was lying here with a rough and tumble man who saw shapes in clouds. "You always find things in the sky?"

"It's relaxing, don't you think?"

"Well, it's not a relaxation technique I've used much."

He let out a soft laugh. "Tell me, Princess, when

was the last time you laid in the grass like this and relaxed *period?*"

"Okay so it's not a relaxation technique I've used *ever*," she admitted.

He tipped his head back, trying to catch as much of the view as possible. "It's always been cheap therapy for me."

She rolled to her side and came up on her elbow so that she could look at him lying there, all sprawled out, looking so perfectly at home. He was long, lean. Wet. His clothes clung to his sinewy strength but that strength was far more than purely physical, because he had an inner strength as well. "What does a man like you need therapy for?"

"A man like me?" He turned his head toward her, smiling as he reached up and pulled a piece of grass out of her hair. "What does that mean, a man like me?"

"A man like you," she repeated, her voice a little breathy at the way he was looking at her. "Strong. Intelligent. Your own boss. You run your own life the way you want, the hell with anyone else, so yeah, what does a man like you need from cheap therapy?"

"You'd be surprised." He pierced her with a look she couldn't quite read. "Do you remember that night at Town Hall?"

How could she forget? "Yes."

"The kiss. Do you remember the kiss?"

Only every living second.

"Yeah," he said to her silence. "I thought so. Look, we both walked away that night telling ourselves that *that* was as far as this would go."

"I know." He was lying there, prone and wet, soaking up the sun, so close and yet so far, and for some reason she didn't want to think about too hard, she needed to touch him. She ran her finger over his shoulder, down his arm.

His eyes heated. "This wasn't going to happen again, we decided. Did something change for you?"

Good question. Beneath her finger his muscles leaped. "Well...I liked that water fight."

"Fight? That was a massacre."

"Yeah." She smiled. "And it was so cathartic, I guess I'm feeling...reckless. I want to know more about you, Mac." She was shocked, shocked to the core, to hear the words come out of her mouth and find that she meant them.

"Why?"

She understood the question. They'd both said this wasn't going anywhere. They'd agreed, she knew that, and nothing should have changed.

Except it had. She had this new desire...a desire to know him.

Mac grimaced and caught her hand in his. "Taylor..."

One look into his wary face and she knew. He didn't feel that same desire. Mortified, she tried to tug free. "I know, nothing has changed for you," she said flatly, turning her head away.

"Wait—"

"No. You don't have to explain why you don't want me."

His sigh conveyed volumes. "Could you look at me? Please?"

She blinked up into his intense gaze.

"No, I mean *really* look at me," he said, his voice tight.

Not understanding, she ran her gaze over his body. Over his chest, his flat belly, his— "Oh," she said faintly, catching sight of a very impressive erection straining the button fly on his jeans.

Her mouth went dry, while between her legs her body had the opposite reaction.

"I want you," he assured her in that ragged, almost tortured voice. "I want you more than I want my next breath, but that's all it is. Physical. That's all it can be for me."

"Because of your ex-wife?" She hated the needy part of herself that made her ask.

"Partly," he admitted. "Mostly."

It was a struggle but she managed to look like she hadn't just been kicked in the gut. She of all people understood a true, deep, abiding love. She understood how difficult it was to love again once it was gone, and she understood why someone wouldn't want to.

Until five seconds ago she would have said she was one of those people who wouldn't want to. She still thought of Jeff, still loved and cherished the memories of what she'd shared with him, but damn it, he was gone, and had been for so very, very long. She was tired of being lonely, tired of being alone and desperately tired of sex that only just barely scratched an itch.

Terrifying as it was, she wanted more. "She...left you?"

"Oh, yeah."

Her heart cracked. "And you never recovered."

"Recovered?" He considered that for a long moment. "No. I never recovered," he agreed, and the cracks in her heart gave, breaking into pieces because she knew, she *knew* what he meant.

"How long ago?"

He lifted a shoulder. "Four years."

"Do you still l—"

"Taylor." He rubbed his eyes. "Maybe we could talk about something else. *Anything* else."

"Like...?"

"Jeff." His eyes softened when she gasped. "Your sister mentioned him. Said he was the love of your life." He ran a finger over her jaw.

"Was," she repeated quietly.

"What happened?"

"We were days away from eloping, and he...um, he died. In a car accident."

Swearing softly, he used all his fingers now, sank them into her hair line. "I'm sorry."

Sorry because he'd asked, or sorry because he was the first man to make her remember what it was like to feel a rush of so many dizzying emotions she could hardly breathe?

"Where does this leave us, Mac?" Leaning in, she rested a hand on his chest. "I need to know."

"It leaves us hot and achy."

She spread her fingers wide on his chest, touching as much of him as she could. "So we're not going to..." Her hand trailed to his belly button, and would have maybe drifted further south if he hadn't caught it in his.

A genuinely pained groan escaped him. "Are you *trying* to kill me?"

"I'm trying to feel better."

In a move that brought tears to her eyes, Mac brought her fingers to his mouth. "Touching you, kissing every inch of you, sinking into your body, that would most definitely make me feel better."

Hearing the erotic words whispered with such sensual intent made her shudder. Yes. Yes, it would make her feel better, too.

Now, please.

"But what about after?" He stroked a finger over her shoulder. "This thing won't just go away with one trip to the bedroom."

"So let's make it two," she said recklessly.

"I'm serious."

"It's not like you're moving to another planet after this job," she said with a teasing smile that faded when he just looked at her, his eyes filled with both heat and regret. She forced a laugh past the lump in her throat, because for the first time *she* was making the move, putting herself on the line, and it was scary as hell, especially given she was about to be flatly rejected. "What? You're busy already?"

"Taylor." God, the sound of her name on his lips, in that low, gruff, tortured voice.

And she knew. He was walking away from this before they even got started. Which, damn it, is exactly what she'd wanted, too. Until right now, right this very moment. "Don't. Don't say it, Mac."

"I can't give you what you want." His expression was a mask of torment. "I just can't."

"I asked you not to say it," she tried to quip, and failed utterly. To save maybe even an ounce of pride, she sat up.

While they'd been lying there watching the clouds go by and breaking her heart all over again, the hose had turned the grass into a slip and slide zone. Her shirt was drenched, and so was her skirt. God only knew what her hair looked like.

She was a mess, inside and out, and looking down at Mac, also wet, but looking all the more magnificent for it, she felt a surge of resentment.

Temper was good, she decided, staggering to her feet and grabbing the hose again. Temper bypassed desolation and misery. Temper gave her strength. And guts.

And it was temper that had her leveling the hose on Mac once more as he lay there all comfortable and cozy with his closed off heart and gorgeous body and incredible mouth that had left her aching.

When the icy water hit his prone body, he swore and lunged for her. She whirled to run but he was faster, knocking her feet out from beneath her, catching her as she fell.

Right on her hat.

"You're right," he growled, squishing it flat beneath her with his weight. "That was damn cathartic." He then tucked her body more fully beneath his,

and once again she found herself right where secretly she'd wanted to be.

Under him.

His smug smile faded as he looked down into her
eyes, and indeed, all of her temper faded as well.
Damn him, she thought, swallowing hard when he
spread his hands on either side of her face. Damn
him all over again because his mouth was lowering
to hers, and all on its own, her mouth rose up—

"Oh, my," came a shocked female voice as two
sandaled feet came into view. Peach toenail polish
and two silver toe rings.

Suzanne.

"Hmm," came another female voice, not shocked,
wearing black combat boots.

Nicole.

"Maybe we should go away," Suzanne whispered, presumably to Nicole.

"Definitely going away," Nicole agreed.

And not one of the four feet moved.

With a sigh, Taylor shoved at Mac. With one last
stroke of his thumb over her bottom lip, he surged to
his feet, bringing her up with him.

Indeed both Suzanne and Nicole stood there, gap-
ing, Suzanne in one of her flowery, flowing sun-
dresses with crystals in her ears, and Nicole in a
black tank and camouflage pants.

Neither of her friends said a word, just looked at them both with shock.

Not that Taylor could blame them. Dry, Mac was a most amazing specimen of a man—tall, built and hot.

Wet, he was every woman's fantasy.

Especially hers.

Mac thrust out his hand as if he hadn't just been sprawled over the top of their best friend. "I'm Mac."

"Nicole," Nicole said slowly, eyeing him very carefully as she shook his hand. "And this is Suzanne."

Mac shook her hand, too, smiling, looking totally and completely at ease even as water ran from his hair and down his face.

"I, uh..." Taylor looked at Mac, for the first time in her life utterly at loss for words. "We were...just..."

"I think we know what you were just," Nicole said with a straight face.

Suzanne couldn't keep hers though, and she grinned. "You were making out. On the grass. With water. On your pretty clothes. You even squashed your hat. Oh, Taylor." She laughed and clapped her hands together. "It's so wonderful."

Taylor patted her hair, and Nicole snorted. "Oh

yeah," her supposed friend said. "You're a wreck. Your hair, your makeup, your clothes, everything."

Mac's lips twitched as he eyed Taylor's friends in appreciation. "She looks good all messed up, doesn't she?"

Nicole shot him a sideways glance. "You like her that way?"

Mac's gaze held Taylor's prisoner. "I think I like her this way best of all."

Nicole looked at Taylor pointedly.

Taylor looked away, but she figured by the look on Mac's face he'd seen the blush anyway.

He saw everything.

"You've done it, Taylor," Nicole said. "You've found the right man for you. No fancy suit, no fancy hairdo, no fancy words... Oh yeah, I like him a lot."

Taylor ground her back teeth together when Mac grinned. "You make him sound like a new car I'm thinking of buying."

"Or riding," Suzanne whispered beneath her breath, managing not to laugh when Taylor glared at her. "Sorry."

"He's my *contractor*," Taylor said, and snatched up her squashed hat. It was destroyed. "A contractor who ruined my favorite hat."

"Right." Nicole lifted a brow. "And what was it

exactly you two were just doing? Working really hard, right?"

Mac laughed, then wisely turned it into a cough when Taylor rounded on him.

"I'm going inside to work now," he said.

"Good idea." Taylor waited until he'd walked up the stairs—knowing Nicole and Suzanne were staring at his very starable butt as he went—waiting until he'd disappeared inside to round on her so-called friends.

"Oh, baby," Suzanne whispered. "You've met your match."

"He is something." Nicole looked quite pleased. "It didn't take you long to be the last to cave on the singlehood vow."

"I'm not caving!"

"You were wrapped around him tighter than Glad Wrap," Suzanne offered ever so helpfully.

"And lip-locked," Nicole added with a smug grin. "So does he kiss as good as he looks?"

Taylor swore impressively, making her friends howl with laughter. "We are *not* together," she said. She was not, absolutely not, going to admit that even if she'd had a moment of weakness and wanted that very thing, Mac did not. "He's simply here doing a job. That's all."

"So the kissing thing, that's what...a side benefit?" Nicole asked.

"Don't you have your own life?" Taylor demanded.

"Hey, you butted in on my life on a daily basis when I lived here," Nicole protested. "And when I was falling in love with Ty—and denying it—you laughed at me every step of the way."

"I am not falling in love with Mac." But her heart hitched painfully. "I'm not."

"Oh, honey." Suzanne dropped the teasing note in her voice. "It's all over your face, don't you know that?"

"We've only just met each other."

"When it's the real thing," Nicole said, also surprisingly free of mockery. "It happens like a train wreck. You see it coming but you can't look away."

She already knew that. Damn it, she already knew. She'd done love once, and it had been glorious.

And painful.

And yet...God help her, she might have been willing to try again.

If Mac had been willing. But she couldn't, wouldn't, compete with the memory of his ex-wife. "You guys are off the mark on this one."

She had other things to think about. Such as getting the money together for the next round of renovations. "So," she said with false cheer. "Who's up for a trip to my storage unit to see what antique I can bear to part with this month?"

Groans met this, and Taylor smiled. Friends. If they were all she ever had, it would be enough.

She'd make it enough.

9

INSIDE, MAC LOOKED AROUND for something to get busy with. Something that would take his mind off the one incredibly sexy blonde he should never touch again. He looked at the pile of leftover two-by-fours from the framing they'd finished weeks ago. He'd asked someone to stack them, and of course no one had. Fine. He could use the distraction.

Halfway through the load of lumber, he was breathing hard but still thinking. Thinking that Taylor was driving him crazy.

From outside he heard female voices raised in laughter. He could pick out Taylor's, of course, though he refused to look. He thought he could even smell her. He stacked the wood faster, but it didn't help. That sensual scent she wore made him think of long, hot summer nights. Of dancing beneath shimmering moonbeams, skin to skin. Of deep, drugging kisses—

Careless, he walked too close to the stack of wood and bashed his shin on a two-by-four.

That wasted a few moments, hopping around,

swearing colorfully. With renewed grimness and a very sore leg, he stacked the rest of the wood, then pulled his T-shirt away from his damp skin. Damn, today was hot as hell.

He'd just picked up a set of plans when a scream prompted him to drop them and run to the window. Just outside in the front yard, where only moments ago he'd flattened Taylor to the ground and pressed his body to hers, were the three women.

Two of them were screaming in terror, not that they were facing any danger to make them scream like that. Not unless you counted one dangerous to his mind and heart Taylor Wellington, who, with a particularly evil laugh, lifted the hose.

He was certain she had no earthly clue how she looked, hair wild, skin glowing and damp, and her smile...it wrecked him. She looked wet, and mischievous, and sexy as hell, which didn't help his disposition any.

She leveled the hose on Suzanne and Nicole.

Within seconds the three of them were drenched, and catfighting like Mac hadn't seen since he'd cancelled cable the year before.

Like a very weak male, he pressed closer to the window. Nicole grabbed the hose from a huffy Taylor, and he raised a brow. Suzanne went down on her butt with a squeal, and he winced. And when she got right back up with a warlike shriek, he could only shake his head.

Then Nicole tackled both Taylor and Suzanne to the grass and rolled them around in a tangle of limbs.

Mac had his nose pressed to the glass now, and he was quite certain he shouldn't be hard as a rock watching them go at it.

And when they finally dropped the hose and fell to the ground laughing like goons, he had to take a deep breath. They'd gotten it out of their system. Good, he could work now.

Then Taylor laughed at something Nicole said. Laughed and looked...happy, Mac realized with a sudden hitch in his gut. So carelessly happy with her clothes clinging to her, her eyes bright with humor.

And nothing like the image he'd had of her when they'd first met. That bothered him, too, how much he wanted to cling to that other Taylor, because then he wouldn't be so attracted.

There had been a time in his life when he'd wanted nothing more than a deep, abiding love. A family. He'd wanted it all, but that had passed.

Ariel had made certain of it.

Now he didn't need that kind of a connection in his life. He didn't need anyone.

But as if she could feel him and his conflicted thoughts, Taylor turned and looked right at him.

Gazes connected. Held.

And Mac stopped breathing.

After a long moment, she turned away, leaving him to let out a slow breath.

Nope, he didn't need anyone. Not ever again.

MAC SPENT the next week working like a dog on the woodworking portion of the job—normally his favorite part—thinking it should dispel the feel of Taylor in his arms, the taste of her in his mouth.

Should, but didn't. He spent every night at his kitchen table, trying not to look at the mountain of bills, drafting up the plans for his own renovation, hoping he got approval for one of the bids he had out there in order to pay for it.

By the end of the next week, he still hadn't heard from the town council, and the stress level was rising. He went to work early on Friday, thinking a little manual labor might help.

Taylor's car wasn't out front, but in a town like South Village, where a parking spot was more prized than the actual car, that didn't mean much.

But Taylor, the moneyless princess, was still very much a princess in that way. She wanted her car parked right out front, and more times than not, she actually managed it.

Mac figured once a princess, always a princess.

He, on the other hand, had to park a good three blocks away, even though it was still practically the crack of dawn.

The building was silent. Letting himself in with the key Taylor had given him, he walked up the stairs. They'd come so far in all these weeks. They were working in the apartment across from Taylor's today, putting in kitchen cabinets, and for a moment he let himself relish all they'd done up to this point.

The place was looking good, really good. With all the wood trim, brick and wood accents, the natural charm and personality of the old building was shining through.

He put on his tool belt because he liked the weight of it, and because he liked the work. He wasn't, and never would be, a Cadillac contractor, someone who ran a job and yet never picked up a hammer.

He wanted to lift a hammer. Hell, he wanted to do it all.

He looked around for the plans, and remembered he'd left them in Taylor's room when he'd been with the painter. A glance at his watch reminded him it wasn't quite seven.

Taylor Wellington was not a morning person.

He'd learned this. Though she always appeared by eight, perfectly dressed and perfectly made-up, looking stunning as usual, she rarely spoke until she'd walked across the street to the coffee house and purchased a very large coffee.

Mac enjoyed watching the process, though he'd cut out his tongue before admitting it to her. Except for business, they hadn't spoken since the water fight. He told himself that was a good thing.

Letting himself into her apartment was easy, he had a key for that, too. But walking into her bedroom, where he'd left the plans, wasn't quite as simple. There were scents in there, scents of soap, perfume...and the woman who wore them. There were clothes, perfectly folded as always, but clothes that made his fingers itch to touch. And then there was the bed, with the luxurious sheets and fluffy pillows that made him want to climb on, jerk her close and mess up both the woman and the bed.

Those luxurious sheets started moving, and were tossed aside as Taylor sat straight up. Her hair was wild, she wore no makeup, and nearly no clothes.

What she *did* have on made him swallow real hard. It appeared to be a teddy, all pale yellow lace. The teeny tiny straps had fallen off both shoulders, rendering gravity his greatest ally as the generous curves of her breasts nearly spilled out, until she put a hand to her chest. "Mac?"

"I...I'm sorry."

She just blinked.

He knew he should spin around and walk out the door, but he couldn't quite feel his feet. "I didn't think you were home."

Another slow blink.

Oh God. *Go, just start walking. Do the noble thing here, Ace, and get the hell out.* "Your car isn't out front."

With a huge yawn, she raised her arms over her head and stretched, allowing the lace to slip another fraction of an inch.

His heart nearly came right out of his chest. "Uh..." He waggled a finger in the direction of her chest. "Your pjs...they're falling." Oh man, she was incredible, all soft and glowing and rosy from sleep. She stretched and yawned again, her legs shifting, pulling the sheet down to her thighs. The little—and the key word here was *little*—nightie barely covered her panties.

If she was even wearing any.

The thought made it difficult to breathe, as every ounce of blood in his body headed for parts south.

Another stretch from the princess, and this time she added a little moan of pleasure at the feeling of her muscles loosening. The sheet fell all the way off, and her creamy thighs came into view, along with the smallest peekaboo hint of matching yellow lace between them.

Mac nearly moaned, too. Was she teasing him on purpose? And was that the morning chill making her nipples pout up against the lace, or something else, something like...*him?* Be professional, he told himself. Get out. Now. He even backed up a step, but then his feet stopped working. "Taylor."

"Hmm?" She yawned, eyes closed.

His eyes narrowed as the truth sank in. "You're not awake."

Her eyes jerked open. Her body stiffened in mid-stretch. *"Mac?"*

God save him from sleepy, sexy-as-hell, scantily-clad women so early in the morning, when his resistance was already down. All the way to zero down.

He had to give her credit though, as her eyes cleared from dream to reality. She didn't screech. She didn't dive back under the covers. Not Taylor Wellington. Instead, she slid out of the bed and crossed her arms.

Though he did top her by several inches, she managed to look down her nose at him. "You."

"I'm sorry. I—"

She turned from him and headed toward the bathroom.

And the words backed up in his throat, because her nightie dipped down in back to the curves of twin sweet cheeks, the thin lace clinging to every inch.

Then the bathroom door shut, cutting off the view. He had to shake his head, hard. "Taylor." He put his hands on the wood. "I didn't know you were still here."

"We've been working together for how long now, Mac?"

Her conversational tone confused him. "A long time."

"Yes, a long time," she said calmly through the door. "And have I done anything, anything at all, that would give you reason to think that I'm a morning person?"

"Uh...no."

"Have I ever gotten out of bed before I had to?"

Her voice was so even. Was she mad or not? "No, but—"

"You know what I thought when I opened my eyes and saw you, Mac? I thought you were part of my dream. It was a good one," she added, and just her voice made him hard.

"I—"

"You should have just joined me, instead of standing there watching me."

And on that heart-stopping statement, she cranked on the shower, drowning out any reply he might have had.

MIDSUMMER HEAT hit with a vengeance, but neither Taylor nor Mac had a spare moment to dwell on the sticky heat. Mac was surrounded by roofers, painters, flooring technicians and enough laborers that Taylor felt dizzy watching them work.

But work they did, and work hard. Her building, once the eyesore of the neighborhood, was shaping up into a beauty right before her very eyes. Pedestrians on the street, walking to dinner or the theater or wherever, stopped to ooh and ahh.

Taylor loved it, loved every little bit of it, including watching Mac work.

Especially watching Mac work.

He caught her at it, the watching, at least once a day. But she caught him, too. She'd be pouring over plans, over tile samples or even on her cell phone and she'd...*feel* him. She'd look up and there he'd be, eyes filled with heat and awareness.

And reluctant affection.

Oddly enough, for a woman who had spent a decade avoiding such emotions from a man, it was the last that got to her.

One afternoon she came staggering up the stairs to her apartment under the weight of a small writing desk. The thing wasn't heavy, just awkward to carry, and worth a small fortune.

She'd picked it up at a garage sale for a song, and was so happy about it that nothing could dim her mood.

"Don't you look pleased with yourself."

Mac stood in the doorway of her bare living room. He wore jeans that had seen better days. They were faded, torn at both knees and one hard thigh. The soft denim fit him perfectly, outlining every nuance of his lower body. His T-shirt had come untucked on one side, caught on the tool belt slung low on his hips, exposing a strip of flat, rigid belly.

Her own tightened uncomfortably in response. "I *am* pleased with myself." Having caught her breath, she hoisted up the small desk again.

"What's that?"

"Just something I picked up. Do you like it?"

He eyed her slowly up and down. "Very much."

"I meant the desk."

"Oh."

Since she'd been wanting him to say he still

wanted her, she felt herself flush with excitement. "It's circa 1920, isn't it a darling?"

"It'd be more darling in your storage unit." But he took the desk from her, making it look like a toy in his arms as he strode across the living room toward her bedroom.

The bedroom was a good size, but he dwarfed it, and as she followed him in, she became painfully aware of the fact that the only other piece of furniture in the room was her bed, pushed to the middle of the room with a drop cloth on the floor beside it, which she put over it during the day.

"Paint fumes are going to be bad this week," he said.

"No problem."

"The noise and dust—"

"It's no problem," she repeated, watching the muscles in his jaw bunch as if he was incredibly tense. Why was that? If he wanted her half as badly as she wanted him, well, then, that was his own damn fault.

"I heard Nicole and Suzanne offer you a place to stay—"

She held up a hand and forced a cool smile, tired of battering down his defenses every time they spoke. "I'm staying here."

"Look, Princess, what I'm trying to say is that this place isn't going to be up to your standards."

She laughed. "It's never been 'up to my standards.' That's the whole point of the renovation."

"I just think you should go until we're done."

She stared at him when he turned to face her, wondering where this was coming from now, after all this time. Was he starting to feel the pressure, like she was, of being together day in and out? Was he, like her, aching for more? "You just don't want me under your feet."

He closed his eyes, then opened them. "The problem is not about *not* wanting you beneath my feet, but about wanting you beneath me. Period."

An immediate hot current raced through her body. "Why do you do that?" she whispered, her knees wobbly, her pulse rocketing wildly, and all from a look and a few words.

"Do what?"

"Remind me in every word, in every look, that we have this...this..."

"Hard to put a finger on it, isn't it?"

"It's an attraction," she said bluntly. "And for someone who claims not to want it, you sure bring it up a lot."

"I never claimed not to want it, Princess." He stepped closer, so close she could feel his breath warm her cheek. Then his fingers did the same as he stroked them over her skin. "It's just that what we each want are two different things entirely."

"How do you know?" She met his hot gaze. "When you won't discuss it?"

"You want me to discuss it? Fine. I want you in that bed for one entire night—" He pointed to it. "I want you there, beneath me, legs and arms spread wide, head tossed back, screaming my name as I touch, kiss, lick and suck every inch of you. I want to sink into your body and lose myself. I want that so badly I can't eat, can't sleep, can't do any damn thing. Any questions?"

Questions? She couldn't remember, she was so lost in the image he'd just given her. She licked her dry lips, then jerked her gaze up to his when he let out a low and very soft moan.

"Have I mentioned you're killing me?" he asked quietly, running those fingers down her throat now, and very lightly over her collarbone.

A shudder wracked her.

"Yes." Her voice was a mere whisper. "You've mentioned."

"Good."

He turned to go, then speared her with one last searing look. "Next time you want to play with me, Princess, just remember what it is I want."

She was fairly certain she would remember.

The moment he was gone, she sank to her bed, then fell to her back, gaze on the ceiling, fanning air in front of her hot, hot face.

10

THEY WENT BACK to business only.

Then, the next afternoon, when Taylor had been forced by her cell phone to stand outside to get reception, Mac came through the yard, lost in thought with a set of plans in his hands. Without looking up, he brushed against her, his shoulder rubbing hers.

Did he even see her? As he walked away, he glanced over his shoulder at her, eyes hot enough to melt every bone in her body.

Oh yeah, he saw her.

An hour later he came through the entrance hall where she was studying paint samples, and ran his hand across her lower spine to make room for himself to pass.

Her entire body reacted.

Incidental contact?

Nothing with Mac was incidental.

He was *playing* with her, when he'd warned her not to do that very thing to him.

Payback time, she decided. The very next morning *she* acted first, and "accidentally" brushed her breasts against his arm when she leaned over to point something out on the plans.

He inhaled sharply.

She loved that, because it made it real, this thing he wanted to ignore. Whether he liked it or not, what they felt was *real*.

After that, she made sure it happened every time. A touch, a look...

Mac never said a word about it, but he would reach out and brush his fingers over her hair, making her want to purr like a kitten and beg to be stroked. While talking to her about concrete or wood, he'd drop his gaze to her mouth. If no one else was around, he'd lightly graze his knuckles over her jaw.

Once he ran a finger down her arm. She had the tingles for hours.

But they never spoke about it again, never spoke about anything other than the work.

And there was plenty of it. She had the second floor unit and the loft to color scheme in anticipation of the finished renovation and subsequent renting.

And there were also the two retail units downstairs. One for Suzanne, the other for...the sky's the limit. An art gallery, or a unique little gift shop...maybe even a bookstore. She loved books.

But she knew what she really wanted. Just thinking about her storage unit, about all the antiques she had left, the precious commodities she'd collected over the years, made her heart sigh.

She'd gathered these things around her like her family over the years. They were her security blanket. She'd sold some, but not as many as she'd thought she'd have to.

Which led her to believe she really could do it, she could keep that second retail unit for herself, for her antique shop.

The more she thought it, the more she wanted it.

Her cell phone beeped. Looking down at the missed call made Taylor sigh again. As if her mother had been able to read her mind from across town, as if she knew her daughter was thinking of doing something crazy, she'd left a message.

Their relationship was pretty much a series of left messages, which made Taylor feel…sad. Sad enough that she actually returned the phone call.

But the moment she heard her mother's cool voice, she hesitated. "Uh…hello, Mom."

"Taylor! How lovely."

"I'm returning your call."

"Oh, of course. Well, I wanted to remind you I'm campaigning again. My people suggested I get a family portrait taken to circle around, you know, with you and your sisters."

Right. She should have known this wasn't a hi-I-missed-you call, but a I-need-something-from-you call. "Okay."

"Really?" The mayor of South Village, and all-around superwoman, seemed genuinely touched Taylor would do such a thing without an argument.

It made her do that yearning thing again. Wanting to be close, close to someone, she said, "Yes, I'll do it. But getting my sisters to agree might be more difficult."

"I'll get them."

She'd probably offer a bribe, a monetary one. Taylor should have held out for that.

"So. What are you doing these days?" her mother asked, shocking her with such a personal question.

Was it possible she really wanted to know? Testing, Taylor said, "Actually, I'm thinking of opening an antique shop in Grandpa's building."

"What are you going to do with that college education then? Toss it out the window?"

"It's what I want."

"Well, it's a bad idea."

Taylor stuffed her immediate defensive response, listened politely for another few moments while her mother went on and on about the high hopes she'd had of Taylor joining her in politics someday—*politics!*—then found an excuse to hang up.

When she had, she buried her face in her hands. What had she been thinking, trying to open up? Trying to let someone in?

"Must be difficult, having the city's most notorious tough lady as your mom."

Mac, the man—the only man—with the supreme talent of finding her at her worst. He'd seen her without makeup, with said makeup running down her face, he'd seen her first thing in the morning and worst yet, crying.

Now this. "Go away."

"Yeah. Sometimes my family makes me bitchy, too."

She lifted her head at that, ready to snap his head off, but he wasn't laughing at her. He wasn't even smiling.

Instead he just stood there, his eyes filled with an understanding she wasn't ready to face. "I am most definitely not bitchy."

When he just looked at her, she sighed. "Okay, maybe just a little."

His lips slowly curved, but unlike what she might have expected, he didn't say a word.

He was good at that, she'd noticed, not saying a word and yet conveying so much. "Oh, leave me to my bad mood."

"I have a better idea." He walked into her room

like he owned the place, in his customary Levi's and T-shirt, a pencil behind one ear and a set of plans rolled up in his hands, looking tall, leanly muscled and tough.

She wanted to be tough, but just looking at him made her feel soft. Feminine.

"Come on."

Startling her, he set the plans on her bed, took her hand and pulled her to her feet.

He had her halfway out the door before she dug in her heels, not that that stopped him. She tried a hand to his back, but that only electrified her with the heat and strength of him. "Where are we going?"

"You'll see."

"Mac—"

The look he shot her was pure male frustration. "Look, you need a break, I've got an errand to run, and if you come along like a good little girl, I promise to buy you a lunch that will make you sigh in bliss." His whiskey eyes and rugged features crinkled into an enticing smile. "Okay?"

Smiling. He was smiling at her. Her tummy fluttered. "What's the matter with you today?"

"Nothing."

"You've avoided talking to me about anything other than business, and you've avoided physical contact like the plague."

"Not like the plague."

"What then?"

"Maybe more like...a good tall frosty beer at lunch."

"That makes no sense."

"Sure it does. You know the cool brew is going to go down like pure heaven, but afterwards, it's going to impair your judgment."

She narrowed her eyes, not flattered. "Hmm."

He laughed. *Laughed.* "Look, maybe I'm doing this because I don't like to see you sad."

"I'm not—"

"Aren't you?"

She stared at him, disconcerted that he could see right through her in a way no one else did.

"You going to tell me what's up?"

"No," she said automatically, because he didn't really want to hear she was lonely and needed to be held. But just in case he was astute enough to see it, she examined the manicure she'd given herself last night.

"Ah." His eyes lit with pure trouble. "You broke a nail."

"I did not break a nail, nor would I fret over it if I had."

A big fat lie.

"Then you're having a bad hair day," he decided

with just enough bite that made her realize damn good and well he was just trying to goad her out of her mood.

Sweet of him, really, but she wanted to be grumpy at the world.

She wanted to be grumpy at him, too, for reasons that didn't bear examining too closely. "Do I look like I'm having a bad hair day?" she asked.

He grinned, a stunning show of masculinity that made her mouth want to fall open.

She closed it tight.

"Now *that*, Princess, is a trick question. It's like asking a man if your pants make you look fat. Damned from the get-go, no matter what I say."

"Which proves my point," she said. "Men are idiots. You could just say 'you look great, honey.' End of discussion."

"You look great, honey," he said, eyes hot, all teasing gone, just like that. "End of discussion."

"Mac—"

"Just give me an hour," he said softly, and ran a finger over her jaw.

Her heart sighed in a way it wasn't used to. It'd been a very long time since a man had made her heart want to. "An hour," she repeated, and followed him downstairs and into his truck.

She had the uneasy feeling she would have followed the irresistible man anywhere.

11

MAC HAD NO IDEA what had made him do the Boy Scout rescue with Taylor, but here he was, driving along on his errand to South Village's town hall to check on permits, with her sitting beside him. His only defense...she'd looked as if she'd had the weight of the world on her shoulders, as if she'd been unbearably lonely.

It had tugged good and hard on the heart he'd thought dead.

Sap.

Whipping the truck into midday South Village traffic, he decided the next time she turned those expressive sea-green eyes on him, he'd just turn around and walk away.

The hell with walking, he'd *run.*

"Look at all these people." Her face was turned to the passenger window as they passed a bookstore, a theater and two packed sidewalk cafes... The sidewalks themselves were lined with the lunch crowd. People were walking, in-line skating, jogging. "Everyone seems so...focused."

She seemed wistful, a little envious even, which surprised him. "*You're* focused," he said.

Turning her head, she looked at him. "You think so?"

"You're renovating a historical building. That takes focus."

"No, *you're* renovating a historical building. I'm just funding it."

"By buying and selling antiques." He shook his head. "Your talent for such things is amazing."

"Really?"

She seemed so genuinely blown away by his statement that he looked at her, then wished he hadn't. It was the vulnerable Taylor again, the woman who had fears and doubts, and was so human he wanted to haul her close and never let go.

That was the Taylor he needed to stay away from.

But she leaned in close, giving him an up-front and personal view of her with that very private expression. She had a smattering of light freckles across her nose. He'd never noticed them before. In her ears twinkled tiny twin diamond studs.

Sweet sophistication.

Sexy as hell.

And the most determined person he'd ever met. He'd never met a woman like her.

"You don't have to baby-sit me," she said. "I'm really fine."

"You're a good liar, is what you are."

She leaned back in her seat and turned straight ahead, making guilt swamp him. What right did he have to pry when he didn't want her to do the same back? "I'm sorry."

"Yeah. Sorry I'm in your truck."

"Taylor—"

"You want to know what's wrong with me?" she asked, her voice suddenly low and sultry, her eyes suddenly hot, hot, hot. "You want to know what would make me feel all better?" She leaned toward him again, and ran her tongue over her lush, glossed lower lip. "Do you?"

He could only shake his head. "Um...no—"

"Sex," she whispered. "Wild, screaming, sweaty sex. *That's* what would make me feel better."

He tried to speak, but found he didn't have a voice, and had to clear his throat. "Taylor—"

"Just in case you wanted to know."

Just in case he wanted to know. *Wild, screaming, sweaty sex.* Images flitted in and out of his head. He was hard as a rock. "Let's try this instead," he suggested, and pulled up in front of the town hall.

The last time they'd been here together hadn't exactly been a calm experience, but Mac tried to forget about that as he led her up the front steps. They took an elevator to the third floor, which housed the building department.

Taylor was silent until the elevator doors slid closed. Mac had never had this elevator all to himself, not once. He figured the fates were having a good laugh at his expense that he was alone with her now. A woman who wanted—

"I've never been turned down for wild, screaming, sweaty sex before," she said.

Mac stared at the control panel, gritting his teeth. "Yeah. It's a first for me, too."

She waited until the elevator dipped a little as it came to their floor. "Why?"

For a brief second he closed his eyes to the bafflement and hurt in her voice. "Because with you, Taylor, it wouldn't just be wild, screaming, sweaty sex. With you, it would be different. And God help me, but I can't handle it."

She stared at him, then slowly, as the doors opened and people waited politely to get on, she sighed. "Yeah."

He had no idea if that was an admission that it would be more for her, too, or if she was just agreeing that he couldn't handle it.

He practically ran out of the elevator.

"What are we doing here?" she asked as she followed him down the hall.

"Checking on permits." They came to the right office. Without thinking, he put his hand low on her spine, leaning past her to open and hold the office door for her.

At the feel of her, he jolted, and so did she.

Looking at him from accusing eyes, she whispered, "See?" Putting her mouth to his ear, she let her lips brush against his sensitive skin. "Twitchy. We're twitchy for *S-E-X*."

Oh yeah, she was killing him. He'd been sporting an erection since she'd gotten in his truck, and there was no relief in sight.

They waited in line for three minutes and thirty-three seconds—not that he was counting—standing close, breathing each other's air, arms brushing, until Mac was in such a state he couldn't remember why the hell he'd thought being with her today would be a good idea.

It was a dumb idea. A really, *really* dumb idea.

Made even dumber when exiting the elevator on their way out of the building five minutes later—thankfully with a handful of other people this time—they ran into an older couple he knew well.

"Mac!" The woman, dressed to the hilt in a black suit and sensible heels, reached for him. "Oh, Mac!"

Taylor watched with interest as the very elegant woman hugged Mac, then pulled back to smile into his face. "What a pleasant surprise."

The man hugged him too, complete with manly back slapping. "Hey, I was on the green yesterday," he said. "Hit an 82, three under par. When are you going to join me?"

Mac winced. "I don't play anymore. You know that. I haven't played in years."

"Four," the woman said with a pointed expression. "You haven't played golf in four years. Since—"

"I remember," Mac said, a strained smile on his lips. "I'm just too busy these days."

"Ah," the woman said with that same pointed expression.

Mac looked at Taylor, and if she'd known better, she'd have sworn he looked rather adorably panicked. "Well, we've got to—"

"No, wait. We're just heading off to lunch," the man said. "Come with us. Both of you," he said politely, eyeing Taylor with friendly curiosity. He had a look to him, and he reminded her of—

"Taylor." Mac swiped at his cheek, which had the woman's lipstick on it. "This is Assistant District Attorney Lynn Mackenzie, and her husband Judge Thomas Mackenzie."

The assistant DA grinned. "Taylor, what a lovely name." To Mac she said, "And you! You got yourself a girlfriend! Oh, Mac, and you never said a word."

"Uh..." Mac avoided looking at Taylor. "No, I'm just working on her building."

"Ah, a *business* relationship." The woman lifted a teasing brow. "I get it."

"No, really." Mac shifted on his feet, which Taylor found fascinating. "She's a client."

Also fascinating, was the slight tinge on his tanned cheeks.

Mac was *blushing*.

"It's just a business thing," he said.

The assistant DA studied Mac closely, her eyes lit as if she was onto a scoop. "Are you just saying that so I'll go away?"

"Absolutely not." Mac still hadn't looked at Taylor.

"Darn it," the woman said forcefully, glaring at the man with her. *"Darn it!"*

"Now, Lynn, I'm sure he'll come around one day soon, and—"

"No he won't, he's too stubborn."

"Yeah, well...we've really got to go...." Grabbing Taylor's elbow, Mac tried to back out of the circle. "Nice see you...uh...Judge."

"Hold it right there, Thomas Ian Mackenzie." The

assistant DA put her hands on her hips. "Are you trying to hide the fact that we're you're parents?"

And though Taylor should have seen that one coming, her jaw dropped. She stared at Mac. "You're the son of the judge?"

Mac sighed. "Yeah."

"And the son of one of the assistant DAs?"

"That, too," he admitted.

"You are kidding me!"

Lynn's smile faded a bit. "Is this a problem?"

Taylor sighed. "No. It's not a problem. It's...um, lovely to meet you."

Lynn crossed her arms. "Why don't I believe you?"

"No, really." Taylor eyed Mac, thinking she'd kill him later. "It's just that Mac might have mentioned any time over the past few months he was the son of the judge and an assistant DA, sometime like...oh, I don't know...maybe when I told him I'm Isabel Craftsman's daughter."

"Isabel Craftsman, the mayor?"

"Yes," Taylor, said, staring at Mac, who was still avoiding her gaze.

"Hmm." Lynn raised her eyebrows as she eyed Mac. "I think I see."

"Mom—"

"Oh, *now* he calls me Mom." Much more friendly

now, Lynn shook her head at Taylor. "Honestly, Taylor, I've never seen this man before and he's calling me Mom."

Taylor had to laugh at the easy wit and charm, but she supposed she would have expected no less from whoever had raised Mac.

"So why don't the two of you join us for lunch?" his father asked.

Taylor looked at Mac, interested to see if he'd allow this.

"Sorry." Mac kissed both his parents, then gripped Taylor's arm. "We have to go." And he dragged her out of there so fast her head spun.

"Smooth," she said when they were both out on the busy street. "Making sure I couldn't drill the parentals."

"Hey, I was just making sure they couldn't drill *you*. I love them, but believe me, they're ruthless matchmakers." He stopped at a hot dog vendor on the corner. "One or two dogs?" he asked Taylor.

She gaped at him. "*This* is the lunch you offered me? The one that is supposed to make me sigh in bliss?"

"One or two?"

South Village had nearly as many cafés and restaurants as it did people, and most of them were excellent. On weekends, 20,000 people from all over flocked to the streets to experience the food. It was one of her favorite things about living here, something she hadn't been able to afford lately, and Mac, who had earned a good chunk of her money recently, was going to buy her *hot dogs?* From a street vendor? "Two," she sighed, and made him buy her barbecue chips, too. She didn't say a word as he took their food and started walking, she just followed.

Which brought her to another bone of contention. When had she ever followed a *man?*

They walked around the block to the back of the town hall, where the botanical gardens bloomed in vivid, vibrant colors. In the light of day, they dazzled in every shape and hue, and Taylor had to admit, just walking through on one of the brick trails, with the scents and sights, she sighed in sheer pleasure of being outside.

They sat down and he handed her a hot dog. "Ketchup?"

Shaking her head, she took a bite. It was heavenly. Damn, she hated when he was right. "So...why didn't you tell me?"

Mac was suddenly very busy eating. "Tell you what?"

"That you come from the same kind of world I do?"

"We don't."

His parents had just about dripped elegant sophis-tication. "Of course we did, I just met—"

"You just met the two nosiest, bossiest, most inter-fering parents on the face of this earth, yes. And they love me, ridiculously so, but they never sent me away to schools for years on end, and they sure as hell never ignored me, not my hopes and dreams, not me as a person. Not once." He nudged her arm with his, his eyes painfully deep. "That never should have happened to you either, Taylor."

All her life she'd felt like a bug on a slide, people waiting for her to make a fool out of her family's name, people waiting for her to fall on her face. And all her life there hadn't been many to understand what that had been like. Only Jeff.

But Mac...he was looking at her with empathy, too. Because he understood. He understood *her*. While thinking about this, she inhaled every last chip in the bag, and didn't even flinch over the calo-rie content. "What I mean is," she said, trying again. "We both came from considerable wealth."

Some of the warmth faded from his eyes. "I don't consider myself that way."

"Oh, come on Mac, I saw your mom's shoes. Prada," she said with a sigh, licking mustard off her thumb. She started in on the second hot dog. "And the diamond earrings. Stunning. You can't tell me they don't pull down mind-boggling salaries."

With careful consideration, he took his last bite of hot dog. Polished off his soda. Leaned back, away from her, he slid his sunglasses over his eyes as he viewed the incredible colors around them. "I suppose they do."

"So all those times you called me a princess? Why didn't you ever say anything about it?"

"And when should I have done that? When we first met and I needed your job?" He set down his drink and stood. "Or maybe when you were snubbed by those women at the historical society meeting? Yeah, maybe I should have told you then, when you were smarting over what they'd said to you."

Shocked at his bitter tone, she rose, too. "I'm just saying, that as two people who share some of the same experiences—"

"No. *That* we haven't done. We don't share anything." He dumped their trash and took her back to the truck.

She'd expected the silence. She didn't expect him to drive in the opposite direction of which she lived. "Where are we going?"

"You'll see."

"I don't like surprises."

"Well, then, chances are, you're not going to like this," he said grimly.

He turned into The Tracks. The streets here had gone through changes. Like many others in town, the buildings dated back to the turn of the twentieth century. But somewhere in the past fifty years, the neighborhood had started to go. Many of the houses had been declared off-limits due to dangerous conditions. Slowly, with the resurgence of neighborhood pride and the Historical Society's interference, some of that had started to change. Houses had been purchased, slated for rehaul, and were in various stages of renovation.

They made a left and ended up on a cul-de-sac. Houses gleamed with the quaint and charming aura of the old redone.

Except for one.

The two-story Victorian, with its busted turrets, cracked paint and lovely but crooked wraparound porch hadn't been touched, though there did seem to be signs of life. The lawn had been mowed. There was a potted plant on an upstairs windowsill.

Mac parked in front of it. "Home sweet home," he said wryly. "Come on."

The foyer had orange shag carpet. "From 1972," he said, disgusted. "The idiots put it over hardwood floors. I'll be restoring that soon as I can, before I go blind from the glow."

The living room had an ornately carved fireplace, painted nauseous green. "The 1970s were a bitch on good taste," he said. "Green and orange should have been outlawed. I'm going to restore that, too."

The kitchen was a treasure trove of nooks and crannies, but there the cabinet doors had been removed, the edgings painted in black.

"Not sure what the hell year someone tortured this poor kitchen, but it's so bad I'll probably start here." He looked at her from inscrutable eyes. "If I ever get out of debt."

"Debt?"

His expression was grim, and definitely said "back off." Fine. But she resented his obvious thought process—that because she'd seen his parents and knew his background, that she'd assumed he had money. "You're an amazing talent when it comes to renovation," she said slowly. "You need to get into some of South Village's renovation projects. There's lots of money there."

"I plan to. After your building is finished, my resume is complete. I have several bids in with the town council, bids I'm staking everything on."

"So I'm a stepping stone."

"If you want to look at it that way."

"A stepping stone, and apparently a gold digger as well."

He winced and rubbed the day's growth of beard on his jaw.

The sound of it made her belly quiver, but temper took precedence. "It's true, isn't it? You're showing me all this to make sure I know you don't have any money like your parents. That pisses me off, Mac."

"Look, I sold everything I had to get into this place. I think I even promised the bank my firstborn child. I'm feeling a little protective."

Which, she figured, was as much an apology as she was going to get.

"I'm not who you think I am," he said.

She put her hands on her hips. "And just who do I think you are?"

"A man with a trust fund."

"Well, isn't that flattering." Oh, she was *so* out of there. She got two steps before he grabbed her arm.

"Okay, listen," he said to her back. "My ex-wife took just about everything I had in the divorce. There's nothing left for anyone to want."

She struggled to contain her temper. And couldn't.

"But even before that I didn't have much. I walked away from all that right out of high school when I went into the police academy."

That caused her to crane her neck and blink at him. "You were a cop?"

"Until four years ago. And there's not a lot of money in that vocation either, trust me."

"I don't care about your money, Mac. And it's damned insulting that you think I do."

"I saw your eyes light up talking about my parents' money."

"What you saw," she said through grated teeth, wondering how such a smart man could be so *dumb*, "was a woman thrilled to the bone to have met a man who could understand her. A man who came from a similar background, a man who in spite of it is going to make his own way." She softened her voice because suddenly she couldn't keep yelling at him with her throat burning. "A man who can see the potential in something, and want to make it right. God, Mac, don't you see? I saw more of you today than you've ever let me see, and it should have been wonderful. It should have been a joy to realize we're both doing the same thing, taking a piece of history and bringing it back. How you managed to suck the fun right out of that is beyond me, but you have."

Jerking free, she walked to the doorway, and then looked back. "I'm sorry we can't share that. I'm sorry I drive you crazy. But most of all, I'm sorry you can't move on after your marriage." It didn't escape her that she hadn't easily moved on after Jeff. "For that I'm really, really sorry."

"This has nothing to do with her."

"Yes, it does. I'm ready for a ride back now, please."

"Yeah. Fine." He gestured her to go first.

The walk through the living room toward the front door was a long one, or so it seemed with him trailing after her. Silent.

Seemed it was the best he was going to do.

In the living room, on the green mantel, was a photograph of a much younger Lynn and Thomas Mackenzie. Standing between them was Mac, looking ridiculously young. She'd guess eighteen, given the graduation cap on his head. He'd been tall even then, though much lankier as he stood there with his arms around his parents, smiling a wide, cocky grin utterly void of his usual cynicism.

Her breath caught at how joyful he looked.

"That was a long time ago," he said behind her.

"I was wondering what it would take to put that carefree, happy-go-lucky smile back on your face." She faced him. "I bet wild, screaming, sweaty sex would do it." Then she walked out the front door.

When he came out a moment later, he climbed into the truck, stared straight ahead with his hands on the wheel, and let out a slow breath. "That was low, offering me wild, screaming, sweaty sex in a weak moment."

"I wasn't offering you anything." She put on her seat belt and refused to look at him. "And you've never had a weak moment."

"Baby, every moment I'm around you, I'm weak."

She put on her sunglasses, lifted her chin. "You should have that fixed."

"Let me guess...with wild, screaming, sweaty sex?"

"Whatever works."

With a low laughing groan, he started the truck and took her home.

12

TAYLOR'S PHONE WAS RINGING when she walked in her apartment. After getting dropped off by Mac, she'd spent the rest of the day at every estate sale within a thirty mile radius, and was suitably exhausted.

"Need ice cream?" Suzanne asked when Taylor answered.

She kicked off her heels, sank to her bed and sighed. "How did you know?"

"Falling in love is a fattening process, hon. I should know, I've gained five pounds since I fell for Ryan. I could be there in fifteen minutes with double chocolate fudge."

"I'm not falling in love, and I'm not going to gain one ounce over a *man*, believe me."

Suzanne laughed, but Taylor was dead serious. She'd learned a lot today, mostly that no matter what she thought she could feel for Mac, it wasn't ever going to be a two-way street, so forget it. Especially given what he'd thought of her. He'd actually figured her as a...a gold digger!

He'd be lucky if she gave him the time of day. He'd be lucky if...

Damn him, but he'd done the one thing she'd told herself he couldn't. He'd hurt her. She sighed. "I'm sorry, Suzanne. I'm just...tired."

"You've been working too hard."

"Nothing a good night's sleep won't cure."

"Are you sure? The offer still stands, fifteen minutes."

Taylor fell to her back on the bed and stared up at the ceiling. "I'm okay, but thanks."

After she hung up, she fell asleep almost immediately, only to be abruptly awoken sometime later by the unmistakable and terrifying sound of someone trying to break into her apartment.

MAC LAY NAKED on his bed, sprawled on his back, hands beneath his head, watching time go by.

Midnight.

One o'clock.

Two o'clock.

Apparently sleep wasn't going to come.

It was the look on Taylor's face tormenting him—when she'd seen his parents, when she'd seen his place, when he'd been such an ass because she'd gotten so sappy over that picture of him.

He'd wanted her to be plastic. He'd wanted her to

be after the family money. He'd wanted, over and over again, for her to reveal a nature he could hate.

Instead she'd been...well, Taylor. Passionate. Steadfast. And unfailingly, consistently, wonderfully behind him.

Even when he hadn't been behind her.

When his phone rang in the middle of the dark, dark night, it startled him out of his thoughts, which was just as well, since he had no idea where he was going with them.

"M-Mac?"

He'd never heard her sound scared before, and he sat straight up. "Taylor? What's the matter?"

"You, um, left your nail gun here, which actually turned out to be a good thing." She let out a slightly hysterical laugh. "Oh, Mac."

He clutched the phone. "You're scaring me. What's wrong?"

"Two guys broke in tonight to steal some tools. They found me instead."

Mac's heart stopped. "Did they—"

"No, I didn't let them steal your tools, they're all still here. The police said—"

"*You*, Taylor," he said through a throat nearly closed with fear. "Are *you* okay?"

"Oh. Yeah, I'm okay. I held them off with your nail gun." She managed another laugh. "Thank God it was plugged in, because all I had to do was lift it and put my finger on the trigger. It was just like in *Lethal Weapon*, or was that *Lethal Weapon II*? You know the one where they—"

"Taylor." He kept his voice even with real effort. "Are the police with you now?"

"They just left..."

Her voice quivered, and broke his damn heart. "I'll be there in five minutes."

"No. No, I'm fine—"

"Five minutes," he promised, but drove so fast he made it in three.

AT 2:15 IN THE MORNING the traffic was light to non-existent in South Village. There were the people emptying out of the bars, and a few other stragglers, but he still managed to get a spot right out front of Taylor's building.

There was grim satisfaction in that.

He used his key and let himself in. "Taylor?"

The only concession to what had happened was that every light in the place was on.

Which by itself spoke volumes, as Taylor was fastidious when it came to wasting electricity.

"*Taylor?*" he yelled as he took the stairs.

He found her in her bedroom, sitting on her bed reading *Cosmo* and sipping iced tea, calm as you please. At her feet, on the pristine bed, lay his nail gun, the cord trailing to the electrical outlet. She was plugged in, ready to go.

Striding toward her, he grabbed the magazine and tossed it aside. He set the tea down on the floor and hauled her to her feet so he could look at her.

Not a hair was out of place. The blond strands fell neatly just past her shoulders. She wore makeup, including a see-through gloss that smelled like strawberries. On the body that had made him want to beg since the day he'd met her was a long column of pale peach silk that clung to her every curve, a ribbon of it tied beneath her breasts, pushing them up and nearly out.

There wasn't a visible scratch on her, but that didn't mean—

"You didn't have to come," she said. "I told you I'm f—"

"Did they touch you?"

"Of course not. I had them up against the wall. I even shot a few nails into the air to show them I meant business. They were scared spitless, the idiots."

"So you're not hurt."

"I just said so."

Oh yeah, she was still pissed at him from earlier. But so was he. He was pissed because she made him care. She made him want her, and it wasn't just a physical ache, which really got him.

Then, as if there wasn't enough steam coming out his ears, she said, "You can go now that you've seen for yourself I'm just fine and dandy."

"Taylor—"

"Look, I've already offered you wild, screaming, sweaty sex, and you turned that down flat. Tonight was a bit scary for me, and if you're not going to help me burn off some stress, if you're just going to stand there looking like a deadly calm cop, then go. Just go."

"You think I'm calm?"

"Aren't you?"

He picked up the nail gun and hurled it across the room at the wall, where it made a satisfactory crash, denting the brand new drywall nicely, before hitting the floor.

She eyed the wall, then the tool on the floor, now in pieces. "So maybe you're not calm."

Not knowing if he planned on shaking her silly or simply kissing her, he jerked her up against him. "Hell, no, I'm not calm. You could have been hurt tonight, or killed, because you're too stubborn. I told you, damn it, I told you, it wasn't safe to be in this building all alone, but would you listen? Do you ever listen?"

"This is my home," she said right in his face. "No one or nothing scares me away."

"Yeah? Well then you're either a fool or the bravest woman I've ever met."

She looked away, and beneath his hands, shivered. "I'm not a fool. I knew enough to be scared." She shivered again. "But I also knew enough to protect myself."

What was it about her that stabbed right through his heart? "I know, Princess." But knowing it didn't ease his own terror of what could have happened to her tonight. Shaken, he put his forehead to hers. "Christ, Taylor." Still gripping her, face-to-face, he let out a slow, careful breath. It didn't calm him in the slightest. "You're getting to me, you with your terrified eyes and shaking limbs. You with your giving soul tucked behind that tough, don't-give-a-shit exterior. You are getting to me. You, Taylor. Only you."

She didn't shiver again, instead she fisted her hands in his hair, and keeping her eyes open on his, very softly, very gently, put her lips to his jaw. "Thank you," she whispered.

"For what? Nearly getting you killed?"

"They weren't going to kill me, they were just young punks looking for tools."

"Which proves my point. This was my fault. You're coming home with me."

"Yes."

"To sleep," he clarified into her triumphant, hungry expression.

"That, too," she whispered, and put her hand in his. "Let's go."

13

CLEARLY HE'D LOST HIS MIND. That, or with the perpetual hard-on he'd had over the past weeks, the serious blood loss from his brain had taken its toll.

But it didn't stop him from bringing her home to his place. It didn't stop him from fantasizing the entire way about what she did or did not have on beneath that clinging silk. And it didn't stop him from wishing he hadn't told her all they were going to do was sleep.

She sighed as they moved up his front walkway. "I'm so tired."

Good. With any luck she'd fall asleep. Like now. Calling himself every sort of fool, he opened his front door and forced himself to lean back, away from her, rather than bury his face in her hair the way he wanted to. As he shut the door behind them, Taylor turned to him, reached up, cupped the back of his neck in her palm and pulled his mouth to hers.

So much for going to sleep.

She danced the very tip of her tongue along the crease in his lips, and with a groan, he let her in. He could do nothing else. It was hot, combustive, and so instantly out of control he staggered back, slamming them both against the front door.

Laughing breathlessly, Taylor tried to climb up his body, raining little hot kisses over his face as she went. "Here, Mac?"

"No." He was shaking with the need to hold her, *shaking*. He led her to his bedroom and gestured her in.

Afraid of more mindless kisses, he stayed by the door.

Taylor went straight for the bed, kneeled on the mattress and turned to him with a sexy little smile that shot straight to his gut.

And parts south.

But at the sight of him against the door—he was gripping the handle tight behind him like it was his anchor—her smile faded. "I thought you were going to comfort me."

"You're going to be fine." It was himself he was worried about at the moment. She hadn't changed from her peach silk, but had added a matching robe that she'd allowed to fall open.

As he watched, she shrugged it off, leaving her shoulders bare, leaving her body bare except for that column of silk and the ribbon beneath her breasts.

Crossing her arms, she ran her hands up and down her arms, and shivered. "It cooled off tonight."

Had it? He was hot as hell, sweating just watching her.

When she shivered again, he sighed the sigh of a man facing the guillotine and took an instinctive step toward her. Suddenly his knees were brushing up against the mattress.

Taylor dropped her arms to her sides. The bodice of her gown dipped low, exposing the alluring, soft curves of her breasts. Her nipples pressed against the silk, begging for the attention he was dying to give. The material clung to her belly, her hips, her thighs, molding and outlining every part of her that he'd been dying to touch, taste, since he'd first seen her.

"Warm me up," she whispered.

His hands slid to her hips before he could stop himself. "Taylor—"

"No, don't think. Just touch me." Another shiver wracked her frame, and when he looked into her eyes, he realized she wasn't nearly as calm as she'd pretended to be. In those green, green depths he saw her lingering fear and horror, and his heart clenched again.

"Please?" she whispered, wrapping her arms around his neck.

He lifted a hand, skimming his thumb over her jaw. "Comfort sex, Taylor? Is that going to work for us?"

Pressing that mind-blowing body to his, she arched just a little, enough to make him lose his train of thought and nearly drive him to his knees. "Definitely, it's going to work for us."

"But—"

She put her mouth to his, and he lost himself in the kiss. "Wanting you like this," she said when they finally came up for air, their lips separating with a little suction noise that made him want more, "isn't a life-and-death decision, Mac. It's just...quenching a thirst."

A sigh escaped him while his hands slid up and down her back. "And afterwards...you won't be thirsty anymore?"

"Not if you do it right." She put her mouth to the corner of his and nibbled some more. "Do you know how to do it right, Mac?"

"I think I can fumble around and figure it out." As it was useless to resist, he gave in, telling himself this was simply a one time deal. *Comfort sex*, as they'd both just said. God knew they both needed it.

"Well, if you need any help," Taylor teased, letting out a moan when he fisted his hands in her hair and tugged lightly, exposing her throat to his hungry mouth. "I'll be happy to help you out."

Then his mouth captured hers and there was no more talking because she couldn't keep a single, solitary thought in her head except for *more, please, please, more.*

His hands danced over her body, gripping her hips, squeezing, before racing roughly up her spine to press her closer to his hot, hard length. His mouth shifted from gentle to ravishing so fast her head spun, leaving her no choice but to fly with him.

Which was exactly what she'd wanted, it was what she'd wanted since she'd first set eyes on him.

Then he pulled back, staring into her eyes while his fingers played with the teeny-tiny straps on her shoulders.

He wanted her. He'd come for her when she'd called him, he'd come and been there for her in a way no one had in so long she'd forgotten how good it felt.

No matter what they each claimed, this was no comfort sex. Maybe Mac wasn't ready to admit it, but she could wait for the words.

The actions though...those she needed, desperately. Now. She could feel her nipples, rigid against the silk. She could feel her thighs, and the dampness between them, and the blood roaring through her veins. Every single atom in her body was vibrantly aware, overly sensitized and aroused. She was tingling all over, so full of anticipation and raging need she could hardly stand it.

She didn't have to. Mac yanked off his shirt. Kicked off his shoes, then his pants, before coming back to her.

At the sight of him, she caught her breath. He was amazing. Magnificent. *Huge.* She would have looked at him forever, but he yanked her against him, hard.

Hard was good. Bending her back over his arm, he put his mouth on her breast through the material of her nightie, and nearly sent her through the roof. His hand skimmed down her legs, then back up again, beneath the material now. Up the back of her thigh.

Where he discovered she wasn't wearing panties. The knowledge ripped a rough groan from him and a shiver of thrill from her.

If he didn't get to the rest soon, now, she was going to explode. Looping her arms around his neck, she slid her silk against his hot, pulsing, vibrating body.

Tensing, his hands tightened on her. "Taylor…"

"Yes," she sighed into his ear, then rimmed it with her tongue, making him groan and his body jerk. Encouraged, she slid her tongue down the side of his throat, thrilling to the way his fingers dug into her hips.

"Condom," he growled, frustration pouring off him. "I don't have a—"

"I do." She pulled back, giving him a small, secret smile as she stroked her fingers over her own breast. "I tucked one right in here."

His mouth fell open as if he needed it that way just to breathe.

"Are you going to get it?" she asked, the words barely out of her mouth before he yanked on the ribbon beneath her breasts, spilling them free. As the nightie fell away, he found the small foil packet.

Scooping it up, he stared at it. "You packed a condom."

"I believe in safe sex."

"Yes, but..." Now he looked at her; hot and bothered, and baffled. An irresistible combination. "When you called," he said slowly. "You were so scared—"

"I was."

"But when I got there you were dressed, with your hair and makeup done. Waiting for me. You...you knew we were going to do this," he accused, his eyes narrowing.

"I knew you would come," she said truthfully. "I

also knew only you would make it better. Only you, Mac."

He groaned again, and she didn't know if it was from getting his first good look at her naked body, or that he was trying to garner the strength to push her away. On the off chance he could muster enough to do it, she wrapped her arms around his neck, her legs around his waist and tugged backward so that she fell on her back on the mattress and he fell over her.

"Damn it," he grated out, lifting his weight off her. "I'll hurt you."

"I'm not fragile." Arching her hips, she brushed the very center of herself over his erection, making him hiss out a breath. "I'm not going to break."

He ripped open the little packet while she ran her fingernails down his belly, smiling when he tensed at the teasing caress and dropped the condom. Twice. Then his hands tightened on her bare thighs, pushing them open so that she was spread out for him, and her smile faded, replaced by a bated breath as she closed her eyes and waited for him to put the condom on, to thrust home.

When he didn't, she opened her eyes. He was staring down at her. "You are the sexiest thing I've ever seen," he said in a reverent whisper. Still holding her gaze, he skimmed his hands down her thighs until his thumbs met at her creamy center. Slowly, so maddeningly slowly she thought she would die, he gently traced them over her, lightly, up and down. Down and up. Her hips ground helplessly, and when he did it again, then yet again, she let out a helpless whimper.

"So wet," he whispered, dropping his gaze now to watch what he was doing, slipping a finger into her as he continued to apply pressure to just the right spot with his thumb.

Her body strained, and the wordless demand she made was most definitely a cry for more.

Still watching as his fingers drove her to the edge, he made a sound, too, a deep, throaty moan.

And then drew away.

With a desperate sob, Taylor arched her hips upward. If he stopped now...

"Shh." He slid his body off the bed until he was kneeling on the floor, his broad shoulders wedged between her thighs. Sliding his hands beneath her undulating hips, he held her still.

She couldn't move, she couldn't breathe... "Mac..."

"I know, baby. I know." And he put his mouth on her.

At the first silken stroke of his tongue she nearly burst right out of her own skin. At his second stroke, her back went rigid. Gripping handfuls of his sheets in her fists, she mindlessly ground her hips in spite of the hold he had on her.

"Good?" he lifted his head to ask.

She throbbed. Ached. Quivered. *"Good."*

He bent his head again and sucked her into his mouth, making her come in a blinding, thrashing, gut-wrenching rush. It was like nothing she'd ever experienced, it was completely out of her realm, and as he didn't stop, she kept coming.

Gradually, with gentle kisses and wordless murmurs, he brought her down, and when her breathing slowed, he leisurely made his way back up her body, using that wonderful, talented, greedy mouth.

"Oh, Mac," she sighed with a last shudder, and kissed him.

Mac could have drowned in that kiss, and might have if he hadn't been so consumed with the sheer primal lust ripping through his body. "Condom," he managed, and held it up. "Gotta get it on."

"I'll do it."

"Just do it quick."

Her fingers on him nearly took him right over, and when she stopped to swirl her thumb over the tip of him, he could only growl her name, on the very thin edge of control. He couldn't help it, not after watching her come apart for him, not with the taste of her still on his lips. He'd wanted to make her shudder and gasp and cry out his name, and he'd done that. Now he wanted to do it again. He wanted her writhing beneath him. He wanted to see her, wanted to hear more of those mind-blowingly sexy little whimpers and panting entreaties.

"Now," she ordered, wrapping her fingers around the full length of him, guiding him to her. "Now."

With one thrust, he drove himself home, and then, overcome by the tight, wet heat surrounding him, by her hands gliding mindlessly up and down his back, by the long, ragged sigh that escaped her lips, he went utterly still before he lost it too fast.

"Please," she begged, those perfectly lacquered fingernails digging into his butt.

Oh yeah, he'd *please*. He let himself go, gave in to the tense, quivering, straining muscles that wanted to ride, and when she dug those nails in again, his hips started to piston madly, pounding into her, possessing, taking. Giving.

Tossing back her head, Taylor arched into him, pulling her legs back, taking even more of him, deeper, meeting him thrust for thrust.

Damp flesh slapped against damp flesh. Breathing came hard and uneven. The mattress creaked, the headboard hit the wall in a rhythm set by their desperate motions. It was the wild, screaming, sweaty sex she'd been tormenting him with for days.

Then, skin slick, chest heaving, Taylor cried out, gripping him for all she was worth as she splintered into a thousand pieces in his arms, shuddering, shuddering, her inner muscles clenching him so tight he could do nothing but hold on tight and follow her over.

They collapsed into each other, still quivering, still gasping, exhausted in their utter satisfaction.

Mac knew he needed to shift his weight, that he was heavy, but he was wrung out, panting for air, and still so entwined with Taylor he had no idea where her body began and his ended.

Several minutes passed like that, while he caught his breath and waited for his world to stop spinning.

"I can't see," Taylor finally said, voice hoarse.

With great effort he lifted his face from where it was plastered to the side of her neck. He had her hair in his mouth. Spitting it out, he said, "Your eyes are closed."

"Oh." She gave that some thought. Without opening them, she said, "And I can't feel my toes."

Craning his neck, he looked at her bare, very sexy toes. "I think it's because I'm heavy."

But when he would have moved off her, she tightened her fingers, which were still embedded in his butt. "Don't," she whispered, hugging him tight. "Not yet."

"You'll suffocate." With a huge effort, he heaved himself up to his elbows and stared, a little stunned, into her face.

Her cheeks were rosy. Her lips were wet and slightly swollen from his kisses. Her eyes were soft, void of that usual cool haze, and smiling at him.

She was so beautiful it took his breath. "Taylor..."

She slapped his butt. "Anyone ever tell you you're pretty good at that wild, screaming, sweaty sex stuff?"

"*Pretty* good?"

The female smile turned quite smug. "Okay. Pretty, *pretty* good." Her hips rocked, just a very little, tiny motion, but he felt it all the way to his toes.

Still hard within her, he thrust back.

Smugness vanished as she gasped.

He thrust again.

Her mouth fell open now, her eyes glazing over. "Mac? Again?"

"I have to upgrade 'pretty, pretty good' to 'mind-blowingly amazing,' don't I?"

Her breath caught when he dipped down and kissed a breast. "O-okay."

Another slow, rocking thrust.

And then again.

Taylor arched up, tighter than a drawn bow, her nipples beaded in two hard buds, her skin glowing and damp as he watched her fight to take what he held just out of her reach. "Oh, Mac. Faster. Harder."

He gave her harder but held back on the faster. Kept it slow until she was clutching at him, mindless again, on the very edge. "Mac!"

Just as it always had been, resisting her took every bit of control he had. "Is it pretty, pretty good?" he whispered.

"It's... Oh, Mac..."

"Easy," he whispered, running hot, openmouthed kisses down her throat. "We're going to take it nice and easy this time."

"No, I...*please*...it's..." She opened her eyes on his, and he could tell by the desperation and need warring on her face she couldn't remember what he wanted to hear.

"Mind-blowingly amazing," he said, helping her. Then stroked a thumb right above where they were joined.

She bucked beneath him. "Mind-blowingly...oh, yeah, it is," she managed as he slowly, slowly thrust into her. "Mind-blowingly amazing." And when he stroked his thumb again, her thighs and belly went taut. She held him in a death vise, suspended for a long heartbeat...staring up at him with wide, passion-dazed eyes as she let go, letting him watch her fall.

The honesty nearly killed him, and took him over, too. He let go, giving himself so completely he had no idea how he was going to ever get over it. Over her.

No idea at all.

14

TAYLOR AWOKE as dawn broke and discovered two things. One, Mac was a serious pillow hog, and two, he slept like the living dead.

That worked in her favor, as she needed a moment to digest things, and she couldn't do that with him wrapped around her like a cocoon.

Gently as she could, she slid out from the two strong, warm arms holding her captive against his chest. They must have been sleeping like that for awhile, as her face was stuck to his chest, her chest to his belly.

Lifting her head, she stared down into his face.

Eyes closed, breathing deeply, he didn't budge.

But there was the matter of his thigh, which he'd thrown over her body and was acting as a weight to keep her in place. Wriggling, she managed to turn from her side to her back, but his leg still pinned her. From her back, she rolled again.

And fell off the bed with a thump loud enough to wake the people of China.

But not one Thomas Mackenzie.

Popping back up, she stared at him, but other than a little moan of protest at the loss of her body heat, he didn't so much as flicker an eye.

She didn't know whether to be insulted or grateful, but settled on grateful. Padding naked to the bathroom, she gazed critically into the mirror and tried not to wince. What was it about wild, screaming, sweaty sex that so ruined a good hairdo? She fixed that quickly enough, and did the best she could with water and soap—so rough on her skin!—to get rid of the mascara beneath her eyes.

Mac was still asleep when she came back out. Slipping into his shirt, she went to the window and watched the sun rise over South Village. It came in slow waves of brilliant orange, yellow and red, probably from the smog, but it still took her breath.

"Hey." Accompanying this gruff, sexy voice came two nice and toasty arms, encircling her from behind.

"Hey yourself," she said, trying not to sigh with pleasure.

"Maybe you somehow missed how early it is."

She let herself go, closing her eyes, leaning back into the hard strength holding her. There was just something about a man's voice in the morning that made her want to melt. "No."

His mouth brushed her temple in a gesture so

tender, so sweet, it made her want to cry. "Tell me what's wrong," he said quietly.

What was wrong? Only everything. And because of it, she couldn't speak, she'd gone mute around the football-size lump in her throat.

His lips cruised to her ear while his hands criss-crossed in front of her to smooth up and down her arms. "Regrets already?"

God, she loved his touch. It was...comforting. He didn't touch her breasts or between her legs, he didn't thrust his pelvis against her butt. None of the things she'd have expected of a normal, hot-blooded male first thing in the morning, looking to get lucky.

And emotion swamped her, drowning her. She was deathly afraid it was *deep* emotion, and maybe even an emotion that began with the letter *L.*

"Talk to me, Princess."

She drew a deep breath and watched the sun bursting a myriad of colors on the blooming day. After the night they'd had, she should be sleepy, but she was wide awake.

And it had been quite a night. They'd had only that one condom, but it hadn't mattered. They'd explored other options, pleasuring each other by touch, by mouth, leaving her little more than a sensory creature, fed on passion and hunger until they'd exhausted themselves.

Mac didn't say anything, but he kept on touching her, lightly, sweetly, sharing his heat.

"I haven't had a night like that since...well." She sighed. "It's been a long time." She closed her eyes and admitted the truth. "I haven't allowed myself to." Then, knowing she needed to say it face-to-face, she turned, tipped back her head. "That wasn't just comfort sex," she whispered. "That wasn't even just wild, screaming, sweaty sex."

Emotion flickered in his gaze, too, but leading the pack of all of it was a sudden regret. "Taylor—"

"No." She couldn't handle hearing him say it, that for him it hadn't been anything *but* those things. She already knew. "Last night I opened up to you, in a way that..." She let out a slow breath and tried to smile. "In a way that, quite frankly, terrifies me. I'm not ready for it, Mac. I'm not ready and I'm fairly certain you're not either."

That he said nothing only fed the knowledge she was in over her head. Way over her head. Throat closing, she backed out of his arms. "I have things to think about, and you have your ex-wife to get over."

Shock filled his face. "What?"

"I've never felt the need to compete with anyone in my life, and I won't do it now."

"Ariel is not sharing my bed."

Ariel. The ex-wife had a name. She swallowed

hard. It didn't escape her that she might be truly and completely over Jeff if she could feel this searing jealousy. God, she'd loved Jeff. But he was gone and she wasn't. "I didn't mean to drum this all up now. God." She squeezed her eyes shut. "We've been intimate in bed, but that's all. That's all it's going to be."

"Yes," he agreed softly when she opened her eyes and waited for a response. Her heart cracked, but what the hell had she expected him to say? He'd never been anything but brutally honest with her, and she had no one but herself to blame for getting in too deep now.

"You know what?" She managed a smile. "I need to go. Lots of stuff to do today."

She figured the fact that he'd silently driven her home meant he was even less ready than she'd imagined.

Still, he walked her in, even though it was nearly time for him to start work. He walked her up the stairs and into her apartment. He walked her all the way to her closed bedroom door.

Then he lifted a hand and stroked his knuckles across her jaw in a heartbreakingly tender gesture. Fighting the urge to grab his hand and hold it to her face, she opened the door and went inside.

More confused than ever.

IN MAC'S OPINION, the problem had nothing to do with confusion. It's just one could never be prepared to have your heart ripped open to another.

It had to do with acceptance. Trust. Willingness.

As in, was he willing to accept that Taylor was nothing like Ariel. Was he willing to trust that she would never, ever, try to destroy him the way Ariel had? Was he willing to open up and share himself, heart and soul?

No. No, he most definitely wasn't.

No doubt, Taylor drew him, and on far more than a physical level. And yet he knew enough to understand that trying again with her, and actually doing it, were two different things.

There could be no half-ass attempt here, he had to mean it. For Taylor's sake.

She'd been hurt by life, too, and he wouldn't toy with her. No, if he ever decided to have another relationship, he'd give it his all.

He just didn't have his all to give.

For two days, he didn't see much of her. Not because he avoided her, but because *she* avoided him. She was good at it.

On the third day, Suzanne came over with a chest of leftovers from a party she'd catered, and informed Mac that Taylor was at an estate sale, drooling over some antiques from France.

"I can't wait until she can open her store," Suzanne said, popping open a Tupperware container. "She deserves it."

Moved by the delicious scent and the grumble in his empty belly, Mac unhooked his tool belt and let it hit the floor. "Store?"

"She hopes to use one of the downstairs storefronts to open her own antique shop." Suzanne shot him a look when his stomach grumbled loudly. Silently she handed him a napkin. "Mini quiches, if you're not too manly to eat such a thing."

"I'm not too manly to eat anything smelling that good." He nearly moaned at his first bite, then sank to the floor and did moan at his second. "You're a genius."

"No, that's Nicole. But I am good in the kitchen. Just like you're good with your hands."

Mac stopped midbite and glanced up in time to see Suzanne blush. "I mean, you do incredible work," she said, pointing to the wood floor molding and casing.

"She told you about the other night."

"No." She sat down next to him. "She didn't tell me anything, she didn't have to. Nicole and I had breakfast with her to discuss Nicole's upcoming wedding plans and..."

"And..."

"And we guessed. She had this…glow about her, and she was…I don't know…*happier* than I've seen her in awhile. Maybe happier than I've seen her ever." Suzanne nudged his shoulder with hers. "She never talks about it, never complains, but we know she's had it rough. We're her best friends, Mac, and we only just met six months ago. Before us, she had no one. I hate to think about her like that, so alone, but even with us hounding her all the time, she holds back. But with you…" She let out a gentle smile. "Let's just say we're hoping she's not holding back."

He thought of the night he'd spent with Taylor. The night he'd held her in his arms, the night they'd rocked each other's worlds with what should have been a simple bout of healthy, recreational sex.

And had really been so much more.

He looked into Suzanne's hopeful eyes and had to tell her the truth. "I don't know what we're doing, Taylor and I, but I doubt it's going in the direction you're thinking."

"Oh." Her sweet smile faded some. "Really?"

"Really," he said regretfully.

She took away his napkin, and then on second thought, took the quiches as well.

"Hey—" His stomach growled in protest.

"Sorry. Turns out I don't have any extra."

MAC WENT HOME to more mail. Mostly bills, which he was making his way through, slowly, methodically, *painfully*. He tossed the entire stack to his table, toppling over the previous stack.

And revealed a thick packet from South Village's Town Council. Staring at it, he told himself if they'd turned down his bids, it would have been a nice little white envelope with a short letter saying thanks but no thanks.

But then again, a thanks but no thanks could come with a stack of other projects to bid.

Hence the thick packet.

Heart pounding uncomfortably, he backed to a chair and plopped into it, his legs a little rubbery. Holding his breath, he ripped into the envelope and started reading.

TAYLOR'S ARCHITECT, Ty Patrick O'Grady, was a tall, dark, gorgeous man with an Irish accent, flashing eyes and a roguish smile.

Taylor happened to know who put that spectacular smile on his face on a daily basis. Nicole, who was going to marry Ty as soon as he convinced her to set an actual date.

But for now, Taylor and Ty, who had some last minute things to go over, were in a meeting. A walking meeting.

Ty grinned at her as they munched on soft pretzels and drank sodas, walking through the lunch crowd along a particularly swank street halfway between Ty's home office and her building.

Using what was left of his pretzel, he pointed at a new upscale lingerie shop. The window display was what had caught his attention. More specifically, the naughty looking black leather skirt, matching crop top, five-inch spikes and whip.

Taylor knew she couldn't so much as afford a pair of panties from the place. How times change, she thought with a sigh that didn't really signify any wistfulness for the changes in her life. She loved where she was, and wouldn't trade it for...well, for all the money in her grandfather's estate.

And yet a new outfit once in awhile would be nice. Yes, she had gorgeous clothes, but all of them—like the emerald green sleeveless dress, matching strappy sandals and wide-brimmed hat she wore to-day—were leftovers from another era.

Those days were long gone, even if her clothing addiction wasn't.

"I should buy that outfit for Nicole," Ty said around a huge bite. "What do you think?"

Taylor laughed at the vision of Dr. Nicole Mann, out of her preferred jeans and doctor's jacket, and into the leather. "She'd kill you."

"Yeah." Ty's fond grin didn't fade. "Love that woman madly, I do."

At the utterly pathetically lovelorn expression on this big, tough, former bad boy's Irish face, Taylor had to sigh. What would it be like to bring such a man to his knees with love?

Hell, she reminded herself viciously. It would be hell, at least on the heart.

She'd come close to forgetting that while lying in Mac's arms, being driven crazy by his mouth, his touch, his voice. She'd come close to forgetting just about everything, including the fact he was never going to love her the way she secretly wanted to be loved.

She'd avoided him. Mostly because she was weak. One look from his whiskey eyes and she'd leap right back into his arms and screw good pride. She'd take what she could get.

Well, the hell with that. "So about my bathroom..."

"Yep." Ty aimed that killer smile at her. "You can have that antique stand-alone bathtub on claws like you want. The floor will support it, and so will the plumbing. No changes required."

"And the window turrets? That won't change the structure of the roof?"

"It might piss off your contractor having to add trim now, but it won't change anything major."

Hmm. Pissing off Mac so he was as unbalanced as she was did have its merits. "How about I let *you* tell him."

Ty, incredibly observant, cocked his head. "Is something wrong?"

"Of course not."

"Mac working out okay?"

"Absolutely."

Not fooled, Ty's brilliant blue eyes narrowed. "I suggested him because even though he's relatively new to this scale and scope of work, I've seen what he can do. The man is magic with his hands."

Taylor stuck her tongue in her cheek. Oh good God, was Mac magic with his hands. "I know."

"But something's wrong," he repeated, studying her closely.

"No, it's nothing." She looked into Ty's worried gaze and managed a smile. "Nothing. Everything is great, you should see it."

"Yes, let's see it," he said firmly, making her sigh. She'd learned there was nothing more protective than a man who was going to marry your best friend. "It's blocks out of your way," she protested, but Ty merely kept walking.

"Well, at least slow down," she grumbled after

him. "I'm not doing a marathon in these three-inch sandals simply because you're feeling overprotective."

"I wouldn't be feeling overprotective if you'd tell me what's wrong."

"Nothing!"

"We're just making sure, darlin'."

They passed by several restaurants that had such delicious scents wafting from them Taylor could only inhale deeply and dream. Her budget meant dinner tonight consisted of a can of soup.

They turned the corner and passed three clothing stores that had her drooling, but the next shop, called Accents, had her wrinkling her nose in snobbery. The "accents" for decorating were all new, cheap and in her opinion, tacky.

On her street now, right across from her building in fact, they came to a flower stand. Before they crossed, Ty touched a pot of daisies. He sniffed at the dozen wrapped roses, and smiled at the lilies.

"Sentimental fool," Taylor murmured, having to smile when he shot her an admitting grin.

"Nicole has a soft spot for flowers," he said.

What the rough and tough, cool-minded Nicole had was a soft spot for this man. "Go for it," she said, her heart sighing.

He bought a dozen red roses and held them out to Taylor to smell.

Instead she leaned in close to the man, who in her opinion smelled better than any flower. "You are the sweetest fiancé in town, you know that?" He looked so shocked, she laughed. "You *are*," she insisted.

"*Sweet.*" He laughed, too. "Well, that's a new one."

"Trust me, these are going to get you very lucky tonight." Then she kissed him, one quick smacking kiss on the lips.

With a laugh, he wrapped an arm around her and squeezed her tight. "Aren't I just?"

He set her down, and Taylor put one hand on her head to steady her hat, and one on his chest to steady herself. Still smiling, she craned her neck and checked the street before crossing.

And went utterly still.

Mac stood out front of her building, looking right at her. Funny, how her heart leaped. Or maybe it wasn't funny at all.

He wore the Levi's with the hole over the knees, a dark T-shirt and a scowl the likes of which she hadn't seen since that very first day when he'd looked at her as if she were the bug on his windshield.

She hadn't seen him yet today, so she couldn't be

the cause of the scowl. Honestly, *men*...she had *no* idea what had crawled up his—

Ty still had an arm over her shoulders as he peered past her contractor to the building behind him. "What a beauty she's turning out to be. Wonder who your genius architect is?" Grinning, he set his cheek to hers.

Mac's scowl deepened, and with delightful understanding, Taylor grinned, too.

Oh, yes, she'd just figured out that frown.

Ridiculous as it was, the fool man was jealous.

15

MAC STOOD THERE out front of Taylor's building, envelope in hand, watching the woman he'd rushed over to show it to hug and kiss another man.

That he knew and respected that man and his work didn't help. He didn't care if Ty Patrick O'Grady was her architect or her trash guy, the impact of seeing them cozying up was the same.

God, he felt like an ass standing there, when only a moment ago he'd been giddy, and hot as hell. He had figured he'd tell her the news, then start off by kissing her senseless, and from there talk his way right up the stairs to her apartment and her very frilly bed.

They'd make good use out of all those ridiculous pillows she had, and burn off some badly needed tension while they were at it.

And then afterwards, they'd go on their merry way as they had before, sated and relaxed, until the next time the tension got to be too much.

In which case he'd gallantly offer his body yet again.

It was a system that would work well for both of them, he had decided, and no one need get hurt. In fact, the only regret he had was wasting the past few days thinking instead of doing.

Bottom line, Taylor had been hurt, too, and she, more than any other woman, understood not wanting to get hurt again. They could be together without really being together.

All parties happy.

Or so he'd thought. But that was before she'd moved on, and had climbed into another man's arms.

He understood, they hadn't had anything exclusive. Hell, he'd made it crystal clear he hadn't wanted exclusive, but damn, his bed was barely cold from the night they'd spent in it.

He remembered everything. No doubt he still had the fingernail marks on his butt from her eager, demanding hands. She'd mewled and clung and cried out his name, and if memory served right—and he knew damn well it did—she'd woken him up, *twice*, with her own hungry demands for more.

So it hadn't been all him, damn it.

Screw it. Since Taylor was still hugging Ty, Mac spun on his heel and went back to his truck. He got caught in traffic, which really topped off his mood, then stalked through his dark house and stared down at his bed.

Unmade and lit by the moon, all he could remember when he looked at it was tangled limbs, breathless pleas and a pleasure so great it had been painful, *physically* painful, to let her go.

It was still painful.

HE WAS GONE. Taylor couldn't believe it. By the time she crossed the street, Mac had left. She calmly finished her business with Ty, then went upstairs, because this was going to require a clothing change. She prepared herself with a sort of adrenaline rush she didn't think she should be proud of. Amusement and fury.

Fury and amusement.

She would wear siren red because it suited her. The matching do-me shoes with the five-inch spiked heels were a bonus because she figured she could always take them off and hit the stubborn, idiotic lug over the head with them to make herself feel better.

Oh, he had some nerve, shooting her that scathing look and then vanishing.

She washed up, waxed, shined and polished, all the silly female rituals that usually made her feel better. Calmer.

And pictured him suffering the entire time. She really shouldn't be proud of the fact she wanted him to suffer.

The sight of his truck in his driveway made her giddy with relief. He was home, and he would listen to her while she told him all the reasons she was mad at him, and then she'd walk back out to her car in her sexy little dress, picturing him cross-eyed with lust behind her, solid in the knowledge that she drove him as crazy as he drove her.

She'd sleep well knowing he was lying awake staring at his ceiling, calling himself every kind of name for letting her walk out of his life.

That's right, she'd sleep well. Then she would wake up tomorrow and move on. And now that she knew her heart worked again, she'd go find a man who could appreciate that.

And her.

He didn't answer her knock. The fury built back up. Ignoring her, was he? She knocked again, harder, determined to see this out.

She simply had to share this anger, or she was going to blow up.

She lifted her fist again, but the door opened so unexpectedly she almost solidly rapped him on the nose.

He didn't even flinch, not this man with nerves of

steel. No, he just cocked a brow and propped the doorway open with his shoulder.

His naked shoulder, because all he wore was a... She gulped hard and struggled to maintain eye contract.

A damn towel. His entire body was pebbled with water drops. Given that, and the fact his hair was wet, too, and she realized she'd gotten him out of the shower.

Her traitorous body quivered at the thought of his long, leanly muscled body in the steam, water cascading down his tanned, sleek skin, his head back, his eyes closed in ecstasy as the hot water beaded over him.

Oh good Lord, now she could hardly breathe.

His eyes, those light, light eyes, traveled slowly up her body. "Fancy meeting you here," he said.

"Fancy that."

"What is it you need?"

"It's...rather complicated."

"Is it? That's a shame then, as I'm running a bit late."

"This can't wait, Mac."

"Suit yourself," he said with a shrug. "But I'm going to get dressed."

She followed him down the hall to the very bedroom where he'd once upon a time rocked her entire world.

Casual as he pleased, he dropped his towel.

"What are you doing?" she croaked, but didn't look away, not even to blink as he shoved those long, long legs and mouthwatering ass into a pair of pants.

Turning to her as he zipped them up, she had a moment to wish he'd shifted around just a second sooner—

"I'm dressing for my parents' anniversary party." A white dress shirt came next, covering that wide chest that hadn't come from any gym, but years of hard labor.

She struggled to maintain her composure and sauntered over to him, telling herself *now*, give it to him *now*, trying desperately to remember all the reasons why she was so angry. But instead of wrapping her fingers around his neck and squeezing, she slid them into his wet hair and pressed her body to his.

He jerked, proving he was not immune. "What are you doing?"

"I came over here to yell at you, but apparently I'm going to kiss you instead."

"Yeah?"

"Yeah."

"Good." Before she could move, he grabbed her,

whipped them both around and captured her between the hard wall and his harder body.

Trapped, she gave one startled yelp before his mouth slammed down on hers. His body was like iron, his hands hard and hot as they slid from her hips to her back. And his mouth...oh, his mouth. All of her fantasies of a down and dirty, knock-out-fight paled in significance against the reality of what was happening between them now. Nothing, *nothing* could have prepared her for the ruthless, ravenous, reckless, unrestrained, raw sexuality of the man holding her to the wall, or her own ruthless, ravenous, reckless, unrestrained response.

His hands molded her body, sculptured her, and only when they were both shuddering, sighing, lost in the driving, pulsing need, did he pull back. Chest heaving, he lifted his head enough to look into her eyes and grate out, "Who are you kissing?"

Stunned by the overwhelming emotions rocketing through her, she could only blink.

His hands held her jaw, his thumbs teasing the lips that wanted his back on them. "Say my name, Taylor. Say it so I know you're right here, with me and no one else."

Oh, but if that didn't remind her she was furious at him! Shoving him away, she straightened her shoulders and glared at him. "I know who I kiss. And if you think I don't, then you don't know me near well enough for me to see this through."

With her pride on her shoulders like a ball and chain, she stalked right out of his bedroom, back down the hall and out to her car. It took her shaking fingers a few tries to get the key into the ignition, but she succeeded, and peeled away from the curb with a satisfactory screech.

It was the only satisfaction she had that entire night.

SHE WAS WOKEN at six in the morning by the sound of a power tool, which really fried her, because she'd only just managed to fall asleep an hour ago.

Furious all over again, that he would *dare* to interrupt her beauty sleep—and she made no mistake, she knew exactly who was down there making the racket—she stalked out of her apartment and down the stairs.

The first thing she saw when she entered the storefront was the antique hat stand, all dark oak and brass. It stood in the center of the room that was empty except for a makeshift work table.

Unable to help from touching the beautiful thing, she ran a finger down the unusual stand, guessing it was over a hundred years old.

"Incredible, isn't it?"

Turning, she faced Mac, who stood in the doorway covered in sawdust. Hanging from his hand was the offending noisemaker, a saw of some kind. "Suzanne told me you're not selling off your entire antique collection," he said. "That you're hoping to open a store right here." He lifted a broad shoulder. "My grandmother left me a few pieces of furniture, most of which I've sold, but this piece I kept because of the beauty of the wood."

"So it's yours."

"No, it's yours. I'm giving it to you."

He was giving it to her. No one gave her anything, or hadn't since Jeff. She braced herself for the sharp pain from the thought of him, but all she felt was a nice warm fuzzy. She'd thought about that a lot lately. Somewhere along the line, she'd stopped comparing the two men, stopped putting Jeff on a pedestal. As for where she'd put *this* man, she didn't yet know. "Why are you giving it to me?" Her voice wasn't the angry one she'd imagined on the walk downstairs, but she felt sucker punched at the look in his eyes as he set down the saw, dusted himself off and moved closer.

There wasn't any matching anger in his eyes. None. Instead, what she saw was a deep brooding that came from sorrow and regret.

He cared. He cared deeply.

Yes, he thought that caring was strictly physical. He thought that caring could be set on the back burner until it boiled over, and then with one night of amazing sex, it could be taken care of.

Until the next time it boiled over.

But he was wrong, dead wrong, and she was going to prove it to him. She ran her hands up his tense, hot, slightly damp arms.

"What are you doing?" he asked hoarsely.

"Touching you."

"Don't," he grated out through clenched teeth when she danced her fingers over his chest. His hands fisted at his sides. "I've had a really shitty morning."

She would have said the same of herself only a few moments ago. "So you'd say you're...worked up?"

"Yes." His jaw bunched. "I'd definitely say that."

"Well, that would make two of us, Mac." She smiled at him beneath her half-closed eyes and squirmed against him, just a little, just enough to have the breath hissing out from between his teeth. "I'm worked up over you."

"Well, that's convenient. I'm worked up over you. I got approval from the town council. I'm renovating two of their projects in the next phase."

"Oh, Mac!" She knew how much it meant to him, and her heart hitched. "Let's celebrate."

His eyes raked over her, hands still at his sides. "You're wearing my T-shirt."

"You left it here. I've claimed it as my own." Backing away from him, she shimmied in a little circle to ensure he caught the full effect of his T-shirt on her body.

Mac caught the full effect all right. He caught the way the torn neck made one sleeve fall off her creamy shoulder, exposing the top of one breast. He caught the way the hem lifted, revealing a peekaboo hint of tantalizing twin cheeks, making him wonder what the hell, if anything, she had on beneath.

She did another circle and his eyes glazed. She ran her own hands down her body. Her breasts beaded beneath the cotton. Then she turned her back to him again, running her hands through her hair. As she did, the hem of the shirt slipped up another inch, showing another flash of her tight, rounded cheeks.

No panties.

With a low growl that reverberated in his chest, he lunged forward, pressing her between the makeshift work table and his own body.

Trapped, she let out a low hum and bent forward, gliding her hands up the table, thrusting her butt against his crotch. "Mac," she murmured. "Mac..."

The sound of his name murmured in that helpless little pant on her lips spurred him on, even as it soothed. She was here, with him, not with anyone but him.

"Yeah." His hands slid up her spine, then back to her hips, grinding her against the hard-on to beat all hard-ons.

"Mac..."

"I know." Gripping the cotton of the shirt she wore, he shoved it up to her waist.

And groaned at the sight of her bare, sweet ass rubbing against his jeans. He could feel the heat of her through the denim, and imagined her soft, bare flesh getting more and more aroused at the friction. Groaning again he reached around her to cup her breasts.

Thrusting back against him, her hands fisted on the edge of the wood table, gasping as he rasped his fingers over her nipples, capturing them, stroking, pulling, stroking again until she was chanting his name over and over, her hips pumping in a rhythm old as time.

He was as close to coming in his jeans as a horny teen with his first erection, but it wasn't enough. He needed to see her face, taste her mouth, watch her go over for him, only him.

Pulling back, he heard her sound of protest and smiled grimly as he whipped her around. "I'm not going anywhere, Princess, and neither are you."

"Thank God," she panted, and when he lifted her up to the table, she spread her legs for him, sighing when he stepped between them and gripped her bare ass in his hands to hold her in place. Her head fell back on her shoulders, her eyes closed, her mouth open.

"Look at me," he demanded, giving her a little shake until she blinked huge, desire-slumberous eyes at him. He rocked his hips, watching those eyes go opaque with need. "Can anyone else make you feel this way, Taylor? Anyone?" Another slow rock of his hips, and another moan tumbled from her lips. "Like you'd rather have this than breathe? Can they?"

"Mac..." She tried pulling him down to her, tried to wrap her legs around his waist, which would have pressed the hottest, wettest part of her against the neediest part of him.

But he'd have lost it on the spot. Instead, he held her still and whipped the T-shirt off her. Then bent to a gloriously full, high breast, whispering her name as he rubbed his jaw along the plump curve.

In response, she fisted her fingers in his hair and did her best to make him prematurely bald.

"Answer me," he said, and ran his tongue over her nipple. "Can anyone else make you feel this way?"

Taylor tried to respond, honest to God she did, even though her body was tightening, tightening, tightening, lost in desperate need. "No." She tried to concentrate even as he drove her toward the very edge. "No one else makes me feel like this." She gasped as he swirled his tongue over her other pebbled nipple. "N-no one. Ty is just..."

He sucked her into his mouth at the same time he slid a finger into her, and Taylor cried out, her thoughts scattering into nothing.

"Ty is just..." he repeated for her, doing something with his finger that made her just about swallow her tongue.

"He's..." She struggled to concentrate. "I..." He added another finger to the first, and then his thumb got into the action, slowly skimming over her swollen, wet flesh. Her entire body quivered, so close—

"You...what, Taylor?"

Oh, those fingers! "He's like my brother!"

He went utterly still. "Your...brother?"

"He's marrying my best friend." Licking her dry lips, she stared up at the man who had two fingers inside her, his mouth on her breast and held her on the very edge of an orgasm in a way no one had ever dared.

She wanted that orgasm!

She was also falling in love with him. Damn it,

damn it, not all the way in love, just a little tiny bit. But even a little tiny bit was bad. There would be no one else for her, she knew in a moment of clarity, it was this man, and as he pressed down with his thumb and wriggled those amazingly talented fingers inside her, it hit her as hard and fast as the explosive orgasm did.

When her breath finally shuddered back into her lungs, when she could breathe again, she released her death grip on Mac's shirt and fell back on the table.

"More?" he asked.

"Lots more." She waited while his gaze met hers, knowing that if she couldn't tell him how she really felt, she could at least tell him this. "No one else makes me feel this way, Mac." Her breathing still hadn't returned to normal, and he ran a finger over the pulse she knew raced at the base of her neck. She caught his fingers in hers. "I never let them." With a slow roll of her hips, she smiled, determined to keep this light, determined *not* to let him see she'd started the fall. "Now tell me you have a condom in your pocket."

"I have a condom in my pocket." He reached into said pocket and let out a grim smile. "This time I have three."

There was something deliciously distracting and

sinfully wicked about having the rough wood at her back and Mac, still fully dressed at her front. Just as there was something incredibly touching about the way he drew his fingers down her torso, followed by his mouth, his eyes closed as he worshipped her body with everything he had. It tightened her throat and brought her back around to the terrifying thoughts of forever, watching him make love to her slowly, thoroughly...and yet she couldn't refuse him, not when he reared up and stripped off his shirt, undid his jeans, then tenderly sank into her, not when he started a devastating rhythm matched with a kiss so sweet and deep she never wanted it to end, and not when he finally nudged them both over so that they exploded together.

When it was over, he fell on her, pressing her into the wood. He was hot, heavy, and she held on to him, wanting his weight, wanting his heat, and wanting it so much she clung, just a little, when she never clung. And right then, still gasping for breath, legs still hooked around his thighs, she realized the truth.

She wasn't just a little bit in love.

There was no such thing as a *little* bit in love.

Nope, she'd gone and fallen all the way.

16

ATTEMPTING TO WORK when one's head was screwed up was a bad idea. All day long Mac passed that work table in the downstairs unit, and like Pavlov's salivating dog, he got a hard-on from just the sight of it.

Taylor had vanished, and he went back and forth between looking for her like a pathetic love-struck teen, and wanting to run like hell.

Swamped by various crews and their questions, he did neither, and by the time he went home, he still hadn't seen her again.

But late that night, she came to his door with a soft knock and a warm, sexy smile.

She came the next night as well. And the next.

The nights she didn't, he went to her. And for two weeks they made wild, passionate, devastating love until dawn, and then silently went their own way.

No strings attached.

At least that's what he knew Taylor would have claimed if he'd asked her, but he didn't ask. He wasn't that big a fool. He could see, damn it, and what he saw was so much emotion reflected in her eyes he nearly drowned in them every time he looked at her.

She loved him. Christ, she loved him.

He was torn between ecstasy and sheer terror.

One night she showed up at his door wearing a siren red dress that made him drool. The back was a series of strings criss-crossed over her slim spine, the front was little more than a low dipping bodice snug to the top of her thighs.

Her mile long legs were capped by matching red strappy sandals with heels that put them at eye level.

Shutting the door behind her, she leaned back against the wood and shot him a little smile that made his penis jerk to attention. "Hi," she said in a sultry voice.

"Hi, yourself," he said, feeling underdressed in nothing but nylon running shorts.

With a saucy smile, she put her hands on his arms and spun them, reversing their positions so *he* was against the door.

With a little laugh, he said, "So I'm guessing *you're* in charge tonight—"

With a yank, she hauled his shorts down to his ankles.

"Tay—"

She dropped to her knees. Gliding her hands up

the front of his legs, she stared at his body, parting her lips thoughtfully. "You want me, big boy?"

More than his next breath, but since she was eye level with the proof, he figured the point moot.

She leaned forward and, as if he were her favorite flavor of lollipop, she licked him.

His knees nearly buckled.

"How much do you want me, Mac?"

They'd been together nearly every night, and nearly every night they'd been silent during their searing, erotic, sexual encounters, unless "harder!", "more!", "yes, God, yes!" and "don't stop!" counted.

So it shocked him when he reached down to pull her up, intending to carry her off to the bedroom for more hot and fast sex that she held him off.

"Remember when you had me on your work table?" Still on her knees, she looked up at him. "When you asked me if anyone else makes me feel like you did? If anyone else made me quiver and ache, the way I do when I'm with you?"

Oh, yeah, he remembered.

She wrapped her fingers around him, and he couldn't quite contain the rough sound that rumbled from his chest.

With a slow stroke that made him quiver, she watched him carefully. "So I'm asking you now...you've had the time to figure it out. Does anyone besides me..." She stroked again, then bent and gave yet another mind-blowing stroke of her tongue. "Anyone at all, make you feel like this? Does anyone else make you tremble and ache, the way you do with me?"

He stared down at her mouth only an inch from where he wanted it most and felt the shock of her question mix in with the haze of overwhelming lust she'd spun around him.

Lifting her gaze, she gave him a smile a little shaky around the edges, and he realized she was not as confident and as in charge as she wanted him to think, not even close. "Taylor—"

"It's a simple question, Mac. Does anyone else make you feel like this, yes...or no."

"Call me slow," he said, dazed by sensory overload as he hauled her to her feet. "But I'm finally getting it." Hands on her arms he looked into her eyes. "You're not holding back on me because of Jeff. You're not holding back on me because of money. You think... My God," he said on a mirthless laugh, and shook his head. "You think I'm still in love with my ex-wife."

"Ariel."

"I remember her name," he said tightly, and kicking his shorts off his ankles, he stalked naked to his kitchen, where he grabbed a tall glass of water for his suddenly very dry throat.

"I'm sorry," she said from the doorway, arms crossed, face miserable. "I shouldn't have pressed you that way. I know what it's like to love someone and then lose them. You idealize them to the point where no one else can compare. I did that with Jeff." She swallowed hard. "I compared you to him, and that wasn't fair."

"Taylor." He shook his head. He let out a laugh, and then another, and then weak for some odd reason, he sank to a chair to laugh some more.

She went from miserable to furious. Chin high, eyes flashing, she whizzed by him on her very determined way to the back door. Snagging her arm, he hauled her down and into his lap, where she wriggled and fought him. "Shh, stop." Damn, he should have put on his shorts to protect himself. "Stop...I'm sorry."

"You're laughing at me."

"Are you kidding? No. *No*," he repeated softly, holding her still. "I'm laughing at *me*, because I'm a jerk. I didn't know that's what you thought, that I was hung up on Ariel. That I idealized her." As it was hard to admit the truth with her sparkling, accusing eyes on him, he tucked her face into the crook of his neck, set his chin on her head and spoke into the quiet night. "I met her at a town council meeting, did I ever tell you that?"

"No. Mac—"

"She was the friend of a friend's daughter."

"You don't have to—"

"Shut up," he said. "I was young, and dazzled. She was sweet and warm and loving, and wanted me for me, and not who my parents were."

"So you got married."

"We eloped. It was what she wanted, and I was touched because I'd told her how I intended to make it on my own without my parents' help, and I thought she was showing me she wanted that, too."

Taylor shifted in his arms so that she could see into his face. "I don't want you to apologize for loving her, Mac. I love it that you've loved before, that you're not afraid to admit it. And deep down, I'm even a little flattered that you compared me to her, that it made caring about me so hard because you loved her so much."

"Really?" He closed his eyes, let out a harsh laugh. "You're really not going to like the rest of this then."

"I'm...not?"

"No." He drew a deep breath. "Ariel started asking about money, wanting me to get some from my parents. She wanted a big, new house. She wanted a new car. New clothes from Europe. She wanted parties. She wanted, wanted, wanted, and started to hate me for not giving in."

"Oh, Mac. I—"

He put a finger to her lips. "I have to get the rest of this out, Taylor, and with you looking at me like that, with your heart in your eyes and your body sitting on my very naked one, I'm feeling far more inclined to see how strong this table is than tell you the damn truth."

"Tell me," she said, and bit her lip, ostensibly to keep herself quiet.

Mac wondered if she'd be so pliant in a minute when she heard the rest. "She decided I had been a mistake, a big one. She went after other men—wealthy, affluent men who could give her what she wanted."

"She left you," she breathed, and her eyes hardened. "Forget it. I am nothing like her, nothing."

"I know that," he said, and sighed wearily.

"There's...more?"

Oh yeah, there was more. "When she picked out the right guy for herself, she ran up every credit card I had, emptied every bank account and screwed me over for the building loan I had been trying to get to start my first renovation project, all as a goodbye present."

Taylor's eyes widened even as they filled. "My God, how could she? She loved you."

"She never loved me."

Her eyes never left his. "And...there's still more isn't there?"

"Yes." Mac's heart started beating heavily, he'd never said the words out loud before. "When she went to file for divorce, she found out she was pregnant. And...she didn't want to be. I didn't want her anymore, but the baby. God. I wanted that baby." To his horror, his eyes burned. "She, um...aborted."

Taylor let out a soft sound of disbelief. Sliding her hands into his hair, she put her forehead to his, offering neither empty platitudes or meaningless compassion.

He wanted neither.

She gave him the only thing he did want, herself. Slowly, gently, she put her mouth to his, kissing first one corner, then the other, and then pulled back, her eyes shimmering with unshed tears. "I want to love you, Mac. Not wild, up-against-the-wall sex, not on this table...I want to take you to your bed and love you until you forget."

He looked at her, *in* her, feeling his entire chest constrict at what he saw in her eyes. Once upon a time he'd have said it couldn't be done, no one could make him forget, but as he stood with her in his arms, as he strode down the hallway toward the bed, he thought maybe, just maybe, she was the woman to do it.

TAYLOR WOKE UP just before dawn, and with a deep sigh sat up. Time to go, just like every other dawn for the past few weeks. The best nights of her life, and she paid for them by having to get up before the sun so that neither of them panicked and felt claustrophobic.

Well, she didn't feel claustrophobic, and hadn't, not once during a single one of those nights, humming with pleasure in Mac's arms, and not last night.

Last night...she'd held Mac for hours and had wondered how anyone on this earth could have treated him as Ariel had. If Taylor had been lucky enough for someone to love her like that, for *Mac* to love her like that, she would have lived every single day loving him back with everything she had.

Her eyes filled thinking about it, because she knew now why he resisted so much, just as she now knew things wouldn't change. He cared about her, no doubt. No one could make love to her the way he did and not care deeply. But that was only part of intimacy, and she didn't see it going much further. They were in Mac's comfort zone now, and there they'd stay. If the only option to her was walking away...well, she wouldn't. Couldn't.

Putting her feet on the cold wooden floor, she went to stand up.

And was stopped by a big, warm hand to her wrist. "Without even waking me?" came his sleep-roughened, sexy-as-hell voice.

He lay sprawled on his belly, his broad shoulders and long, long legs taking up nearly the entire mattress. Only seconds before she'd been right there with him, and she was shocked by the immense yearning to leap back in and snuggle tight.

If she did, if she so much as touched him right now, she'd lose it. "Got work, Slick," she said, and lightly slapped his very nice butt.

"No, you don't." Without letting go of her, he pushed up, sat back against the headboard and tugged.

She fell against that warm chest, and had to close her eyes when she braced her hands against it. "Mac—"

"Don't go."

She tried to wriggle free. "I need to."

"No, you don't. You're running out of here because you think that's what I want." He waited until she opened her eyes, helping her along by putting his hands on her face. "You don't want to scare me," he said in a terrifyingly gentle voice. "You don't want to worry me with your feelings—"

Again she tried to get up. "Mac—"

"No, listen. I have to say this. I had a dream. You were gone." A spasm of pain crossed his features as he held her still. "And I was back to the way things were. Alone. I hated it. It felt cold without you, Taylor. Empty."

"It...did?"

"It's all happened so slowly, I didn't realize..."

Her heart stopped. "What happened so slowly?"

He blew out a breath. "Before you, I told myself I never wanted to share myself again, and that included my bed. I told myself I would never open up to a woman, that I would never want, need or ache for one to distraction."

"I know, Mac. God. I know—"

"But I was wrong. Life can't be lived like that. You taught me that. Only you, Taylor."

She stopped trying to get free and stared at him. "I'm sorry. My heart just stopped, which means I'm not getting any blood to my brain, so I must have heard you wrong. Could you..."

"I love you, Taylor." His smile, a bit wobbly, jump-started her heart. His thumbs stroked her jaw, helping with blood flow. "Did you hear that?"

"I...yes," she whispered, stunned. "Yes."

"I love you with all I've got, and I hope to hell you feel something close to that for me, too, because I don't think I can go through this again and have you not feel it back...." He stared at her, then hissed out a breath. "Could you say something here? Anything?"

She put her fingers to his mouth, and through a half laugh, half sob, put her forehead to his and managed to repeat his words back. "I love you. God, Mac, I love you with all I've got. And I've hoped like hell you felt *something* back, too, because I *know* I can't go through this again." She let out a shaky breath. "And not have you feel it back."

Closing his eyes, he wrapped his arms around her and squeezed so hard she could hardly draw a breath, but who needed air? Not her, she had Mac, she had his love, she had everything she could ever want, forget breathing.

Mac rolled over, tucking her snugly beneath him, pressing her into the mattress as he lifted his head. Sinking a hand into her hair, he smiled down at her. "Be mine, Taylor. Be my wife, my lover, my heart."

His smile nearly burst her heart. "Yes. Yes to all of it."

His lips found hers in a sealing, promising kiss. "So from now on you'll wake up with me? Forever, just the two of us?"

She held her breath, not because he was still squeezing her too hard, which he was, but because she had yet to share her one last, very private, very secret fantasy with anyone. "I'll wake up with you, only you."

He grinned.

And she slowly let out that breath wondering if she was going to get hurt after all. "Until we have a baby. A little girl," she added breathlessly when his grin faded, "with your beautiful eyes and my savvy fashion sense and then there will be three of us."

He didn't say anything and she rushed on. "She'll want to pounce on us early in the mornings, and snuggle in," she teased, while inside she was dying, dying, *dying*, not knowing if he would ever want to have kids after what Ariel had done to him.....

He ran a finger down her jaw, her throat, to where her heart lay in her chest nearly beating its way past her ribs. "You want to have a baby," he said, his voice thick. "With me."

"I do," she whispered. "Only with you, Mac. What do you say?"

He watched his finger circle over her heart, eyes solemn. Then he slowly smiled and lifted his head. "I can't think of anything more perfect than that."

Her heart sighed, completely content.

"Let's do it, Princess. Let's do it all." He rolled with her over the bed again, and then again, until they were both laughing.

Then bent his head to hers to make it all come true.

Epilogue

One Year Later

"THE PLACE IS FULL," Nicole told Taylor, plopping into a plush chair in the bride's dressing room of the church. "We have exactly five minutes to get out there. How many people did you invite anyway, a bazillion?"

Standing in front of a full-length mirror admiring herself all in white satin and lace, Taylor sighed with so much joy she could hardly contain herself. "Just about."

"Mac's out there of course. He's got his eagle eye on this door, let me tell you."

At the thought of him, her heart nearly burst. "Does he now?"

"Yeah, he's looking a bit like he hit the lottery."

"He did," Taylor said, and laughed.

Suzanne came up on her right and ran a finger over the bride's veil. "You look gorgeous."

"You both look pretty gorgeous yourselves."

Nicole sighed and came up on the other side, the

three of them staring at each other in the reflection. "You're right. We don't look half-bad, considering we're dressed to the nines. Why couldn't we wear jeans like we did at my wedding last month? Think how original it would have been."

"Oh, be quiet. The dress won't kill you." Suzanne smiled when Nicole lifted a bottle of champagne and three long stemmed glasses. "Well, that's more like it. Aren't you so sweet to think of it. I thank Ty for that."

"The man did sweeten me up," Nicole admitted, pouring them each a glass. "What can I say, love did exactly what you said it would, hit the three of us like a tornado."

Taylor laughed. "A tornado. So *that's* why I feel so unsteady on my feet."

"You look steady enough," Suzanne said softly, reaching for her hand. "I'm so glad you're happy. I'm just so glad for all of us." Her eyes filled. "I love you guys."

"Ah, hell, I actually have mascara on today and she's going to get sloppy." Nicole sighed as her own eyes went suspiciously bright. "But I love you guys, too."

Taylor laughed, and a tear fell. "To us, then. All six of us." Both she and Nicole lifted their glasses, but Suzanne did not.

"What's the matter?" Nicole demanded.

"I, um...can't drink." She grinned and patted her stomach. "As of this morning."

Nicole's jaw dropped. "You're pregnant."

"Yep."

"Oh my God." Taylor's heart felt like it was going to burst as they all hugged and ended up messing up each other's makeup anyway.

"We're trying, too," Nicole admitted, which prompted another group hug and more tears. Then they went back to the mirror to check the damage.

Taylor felt so full of love and joy and hope, she could burst. "Well then." Her voice was thick as she kissed first Suzanne's cheek, then Nicole's. She lifted her glass. "To all of us, seven for now, and God willing, more to come."

"To all of us."

"All of us."

Grinning, crying, arm in arm they walked out of the room, ready for all of it.

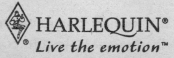

The world's bestselling romance series.

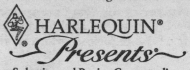

HARLEQUIN® *Presents*

Seduction and Passion Guaranteed!

Every book is part of a miniseries in 2003.
These are just some of the exciting themes you can expect...

Your dream ticket to the vacation of a lifetime!

Tall, dark—and ready to marry!

They're guaranteed to raise your pulse!

They're the men who have everything—except a bride....

Marriage is their mission....

Legally wed, but he's never said, "I love you..."

They speak the language of passion

Passion™

Sophisticated spicy stories—seduction and passion guaranteed

Pick up a Harlequin Presents® novel and you will enter a world of spine-tingling passion and provocative, tantalizing romance!

Available wherever Harlequin books are sold.

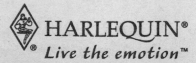

HARLEQUIN®
Live the emotion™

Visit us at www.eHarlequin.com

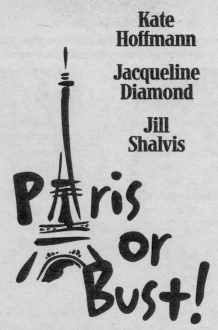

They're strong, they're sexy, they're not afraid to use the assets Mother Nature gave them....

Venus Messina is...

#916 WICKED & WILLING
by Leslie Kelly
February 2003

Sydney Colburn is...

#920 BRAZEN & BURNING
by Julie Elizabeth Leto
March 2003

Nicole Bennett is...

#924 RED-HOT & RECKLESS
by Tori Carrington
April 2003

The Bad Girls Club...where membership has its privileges!

Available wherever

is sold....

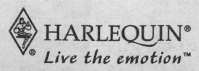

Visit us at www.eHarlequin.com

HTBGIRLS

USA TODAY *bestselling author*

JULIE KENNER

Brings you a supersexy tale of love and mystery...

Silent CONFESSIONS

A BRAND-NEW NOVEL.

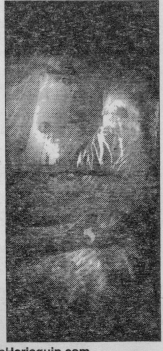

Detective Jack Parker needs an education from a historical sex expert in order to crack his latest case—and bookstore owner Veronica Archer is just the person to help him. But their private lessons give Ronnie some other ideas on how the detective can help *her* sexual education....

"JULIE KENNER JUST MIGHT WELL BE THE MOST ENCHANTING AUTHOR IN TODAY'S MARKET."
—THE ROMANCE READER'S CONNECTION

Look for SILENT CONFESSIONS, available in April 2003.

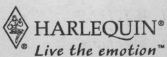